A Dark Shaft of Light

Owen Chambers

First e-publication March 2013

First printing October 2013

ISBN-10: 0957589913
ISBN-13: 978-0957589919

DEDICATION

To Barbara, Tom, Rob and Andy.

ACKNOWLEDGMENTS

My thanks to my good friend Jennie Fischer for reading through the manuscript and correcting the English.

CHAPTER 1

Dirty spray showered the windscreen as another lorry roared past. The driver of the little Vauxhall Nova eased off further on the accelerator and gripped the steering wheel even more tightly. His face was thrust forward almost to the glass as he tried to peer through the streaming windscreen. The rain-laden sky left little light, and the October day was late into its life. He glanced at his rear-view mirror to see the looming menace of a massive lorry radiator, and the bright eyes of its lights. A horn sounded loudly as the impatient tormentor pulled out into the path of another multi-wheeled monster. In panic, he lifted his foot completely off the accelerator, and the little car slowed suddenly. Almost immediately another lorry horn sounded angrily behind, and another massive radiator filled the rear-view mirror. The wind-driven rain increased in intensity.

Tears filled Kevin's eyes, and the fear made him feel nauseous and weak. Through the rivulets of muddy water running down his windscreen an exit sign loomed to his left, and was gone.

"One mile!"

He had to get off the M62. He could see virtually nothing.

He moved so close to the windscreen that his nose touched the glass. The discomfort of his position increased his misery further and his breath began to mist over the windscreen. The exit slashes counted down. He swung off the motorway into the exit lane exciting a further angry honking. He had forgotten to indicate.

The exit lane sloped upwards and a car came up on his outside forcing Kevin to take the first left at the roundabout at the top. The road was narrow and dark. Somewhere beyond the clouds the sun had set. The rain continued to pour down, but at least the treacherous spray had gone and the windscreen wipers were more able to cope.

Where was he going? He had to find a place to stop.

He was now driving at about 20mph, but there was no car behind him. However, the feeling of panic did not leave him, and then came further disaster. Up ahead were flashing yellow lights, a blue police sign saying "Flood Diversion" and an arrow pointing to the left. The road was narrower and led up hill. Then, there came a crossroads with no diversion sign so Kevin drove straight across. The road narrowed further and became steeper, with a vigorous stream coming down it. Just over the crest of the hill the little Nova began to cough and the accelerator began to lose effectiveness. In the headlights, through the driving rain, he saw a gate to a field. In front of it, there was enough space to park. He pulled in and stopped leaving the engine stuttering.

Why was he so weak? He was thirty-one, but had allowed himself to be forced off the motorway, forced on to this road, and here he was - stranded in the middle of nowhere.

As he looked through the rain lashed windscreen at the dark outline of the hedge in front of him a feeling of total desolation swept over him.

Mother was dead. He was completely alone. Only a couple of neighbours had been present at the funeral. An attendance highlighted by the large crematorium hall. A hireling vicar, who had never known his mother, gave an empty eulogy. She had kept herself to herself, proud of her only son and his achievements.

For a moment that thought stirred a momentary feeling of pride. Then the despair came shatteringly back. How fragile those achievements looked now. Professor Thomas had retired six months ago. A young Turk had taken over, sharp, intelligent and ruthlessly ambitious. There was now no place for a "plodding inadequate trapped in outmoded formalisms". Those had been Professor Draper's words, as Kevin had stumbled and stuttered through a presentation of his work to him. He had felt like resigning there and then, but Richard Murdoch had reminded him how difficult it would be for Draper to get rid of him, that at least he should hang on for his sick mother's sake. It had been hard.

For the first week or two Richard Murdoch had born the brunt of Draper's sharp tongue and unpleasantness, but then he had brought in the union, who had spoken of "constructive dismissal". Draper had bought him off by promoting him and putting him in charge of lecture timetabling and student relations. Perhaps Draper's sudden acquiescence was because he had found a softer target. It began in earnest then, constant criticisms of everything that Kevin did. The sensitive antennae of the students picked up on his fall from grace, and the lecturing that had always been difficult for him became a humiliating nightmare.

He glanced involuntarily to the back seat where his leather brief case lay. In it was his letter of resignation. He had had enough.

As he looked round, he thought that he had caught a movement in the gloomy shadows of the trees on the opposite side of the road. His present predicament was thrust back to him and to his despair was joined fear.

He pressed the accelerator and the engine gave a final stutter and died. In near panic, he turned the ignition key, the engine turned slowly over but failed to catch, desperate he tried to turn the engine again but now the battery had no power left and there was only a soft clunk.

Then there was a click. The courtesy light overhead came on as the passenger door was pulled open. There was a rush inward of cold and wet, a smell of damp earth and a strong smell of decay. A human form leapt into the passenger seat. It had on what had probably been a light coloured coat, but which was now sodden and covered in dark brown mud. The coat was badly torn and parts of it seemed completely shredded. The hair was long reaching to the shoulders but matted with wet clay. The face was hidden beneath dirt, only the eyes showed, piercing and cold. Already extreme fright was making breathing difficult, and his breath was coming in fitful gasps. His gaze dropped and in the thing's right hand he saw a small pistol, its black hole of death pointing straight at him. His breathing became shallower and laboured as he struggled for air, then he was gasping like a stranded fish, and a deep blackness rose up to overwhelm him.

He was in a cold shower. Then the image of a white tiled bathroom melted into a dimly lit view of muddy ground. There was a sharp coldness on his neck and he felt the chilled water flowing down his back. He was sitting sideways in the driver's seat, half out of the car. His head had been pushed between his legs, and he could feel the pressure of a hand on the back of his scalp.

"Are you alright?" asked a female voice. It was definitely a young woman's voice, but there was a peculiar croaking quality to it.

Kevin could not speak but he managed to nod.

"I am sorry I frightened you," said the voice with an almost exaggerated politeness, the croaking aspect fading, but a strong northern accent coming through. "I shouldn't have threatened you with that toy, but I was so afraid that you would drive away."

Slowly Kevin raised his head and turned cautiously to look at the speaker. She was somewhat smaller than he was, but nearly all else was hidden by the filthy coat. Her face was smeared in streaked clay. Nearly all features were invisible beneath stains and dirt. Her feet were bare and there were bright red streaks of fresh blood showing through the dirt. But the blue eyes were what stood out; they stared at him, penetrating and icy. In her left hand she gripped an extremely filthy handbag.

He found that he was shaking uncontrollably. He tried to speak but nothing would come out.

"My name is Ella." she said "I am so glad to see you, I thought that I would be stuck here all night."

"What..." stuttered Kevin before his voice failed again.

"I was with some guys, I thought that they were my friends, but they forced me to strip. They wanted to rape me. But I managed to grab my coat and bag and run for it."

"I ran through a stream. More like a river, it was such a torrent. I was knocked off my feet by the force of the water. It was cold, so very cold." She shivered, hesitating for moment at the memory.

"But I got out and into a wood on the other side. They gave up then and I saw them drive away." She added.

Kevin stared; the shock was making him feel sick. He shook uncontrollably.

"I don't want to go back," she pleaded. "Where are you going?"

"Bristol," stuttered Kevin.

"Could you take me? Help me out, please."

Kevin felt befuddled, confused and still very shocked. "The car..." he began "... broken..."

She looked him straight in the face her eyes glaring.

"OK." she said finally her gaze relaxing "Let's try to fix it."

Kevin was no help at all. He knew very little about cars and he was so distressed that he was nearly incapable of movement. Firstly, she led him gently around to the passenger seat, and sat him down there where she left him to tremble. She then tried to start the car peering knowledgeably at the dash. The engine barely turned over. Seemingly satisfied she turned to Kevin. "Do you have a torch?"

Kevin nodded wordlessly and fumbled in the glove compartment and passed it to her. She turned it on and stared critically at the feeble orange light, but she went out without saying anything, opened the bonnet and vanished under it for about five minutes.

"Loose wire on the coil, I think." she declared, as she reappeared "I don't think you're up to driving so I would like you to get out and push. We're lucky we're on the crest of a hill."

Kevin felt as if he had no will of his own. She virtually led him round to the back of the car and then left him there as she went to the driver's side. She opened the driver's door but stayed outside, her hands on the steering wheel.

"OK! Push!" she yelled.

It was fortunate that the car was small and that they only had to push it a short distance on to the hill, because Kevin did not feel that he made much of a contribution. As the car began to move down the hill it picked up speed, Ella jumped into the driver's seat and Kevin found himself being left behind. The car's lights came on and there was a loud cough followed by a roar. The little car sped away leaving Kevin staring at its rapidly vanishing taillights. The noise of the car disappeared into the noise of the wind and rain. He was totally alone.

He was dressed only in the light jacket that he had been wearing for driving. It offered little protection. The wind howled its lonely sound through the trees. The darkness was nearly absolute. With the sense of desolation and abandonment rose a child's fear of the night. Kevin stood there shaking and numb. The wet and the cold seeped into him.

"What could he do now?"

The sound of a car came to his ears and coming up the hill from the direction the Nova had taken appeared a car's headlights. As it came closer he realised it was his own Nova. It stopped beside him. The driver's door opened and Ella's dirty head appeared.

"Come on!" she said, "Get in!"

"Sorry to keep you waiting, but I had to make sure that the battery was recharged."

Kevin sank into the passenger seat. He knew that there was a host of questions that he should ask, even simple ones like whether she had a driving license. But he really did not want to know. There was no way that he could drive. He was still shocked from what had happened.

They had not gone far when Kevin had to ask her to stop. He hurriedly opened the door and leaning out was violently sick. After he had lost his motorway service's tea, he dry heaved painfully a couple of times. When he was sure it had passed he pulled shut the car door and leaned back in his seat. The taste in his mouth was bitter and unpleasant and his throat hurt slightly, but overall he felt better.

They drove in silence after that. He wondered who or what she was, with all sorts of terrifying fancies streaming through his mind.

She seemed to have a good idea where they were going and within half an hour they were back on the M62, heading west to join the M6. In that time Kevin made one discovery about his mysterious driver. Underneath the ragged coat she was nearly naked. He could see through the tears in the coat extremely filthy stained skin. How could she have stood the cold?

On the motorway conditions had not improved much except that there were fewer lorries. Ella's driving was somewhat erratic, but she made up for it with what Kevin thought was misplaced confidence. While overtaking a lorry she pulled out in front of a car which just managed to avoid them, while honking loudly. Ella swore and made a rude sign at the other driver, which fortunately he was unlikely to see. Kevin sank deeper into his seat.

After that the woman did slow her driving slightly. She began to ask the questions then. What was his name? What was his house like? Was he married? Did he live with a partner? Did he have a job?

At first Kevin answered with minimum responses.

Kevin Hansen - small terraced house - unmarried - no partner - live alone.

He found that if he did not look at her, and ignored the smell then he could speak to her as if she were a perfectly normal hitchhiker. (Not that Kevin would voluntarily consider picking one up). And when the topic came on to his work bringing back the old despair then he told her more and more, until it was spilling out.

It started with him saying that he was a lecturer in mathematics at the University of North Bristol and she exclaiming how impressed she was with that.

"Don't be!" said Kevin, with a brittle forcefulness, "On Monday, I am going to resign."

"Why?" she queried, "It sounds like a really good job."

"It was a good job," said Kevin, "But the old professor retired and the new one thinks that I'm useless."

"Why doesn't he sack you, then?" she asked

"It's very difficult for him to do that," replied Kevin, "Since it would have to go to a professorial committee, but life is just unbearable. I have stopped doing any research, and the lecturing is getting harder and harder."

"But what will you do?"

"I don't know. Perhaps get a job in industry."

"That may not be easy. Well-paid jobs are hard to come by."

Kevin stared fixedly at the dash, carefully avoiding looking at her. But he could well imagine the doubtful look that had appeared beneath the dirt on her face. With his character it would be very hard to get any sort of job.

"What did you like about your job?"

"The research, I am a specialist in mathematical proofs. I find it so satisfying when something works out. It is the one thing that I seem to find easy and everybody else finds hard."

"Oh! I have no idea what you are talking about, but surely this new professor still needs a specialist in… Whatever it is?" With her last question, the apparition demonstrably lifted both her hands of the wheel and into the air in a most alarming way.

"No, he is an ambitious modernist. He wants to do experimental mathematics on computers. Something he can take to industry and charge money for," replied Kevin, his eyes fixed on her wayward hands.

"Oh!" she laughed, her errant hands returning to the steering wheel, "I understand about the money. Is there no money in what you do?"

"No, it's a purely academic pursuit."

"Can't you twist it into something that would make money?"

"I am afraid not. I have accepted that there is no place for me and on Monday that's it. He will probably ask me to go straightaway; he has another man in his old college in Manchester that he wants to bring in."

"I have been in terrible holes." she said, "I have even faced death, but I have never given up. You must try to carry on."

"I am not like you, or like most people. Look at me now! I am still shaking and I both fainted and was physically sick. I am completely unable to drive because of it. Most normal people would have recovered sufficiently to do that by now. It's like that at work the new Professor makes me so ill that I can't do anything."

Kevin felt himself becoming more agitated, as his despair over work combined with the more recent fright.

"Are you religious?" she asked surprisingly.

"No!" replied Kevin.

"Neither am I, but I spend a lot of time talking to my dad. That's funny, as I never had one," she laughed. "Better that way, as I can have just the dad I want. No faulty real thing getting in the way. My dad's so comforting. I just have him saying what nice dads in books say. I even have fights with him, like a real dad."

"He saved me from my mother," her voice becoming bitter. "She was a tart and a druggy. She wanted me to turn tricks for her johns. She's too old now and spends all her time watching TV. We hate - really hate - each other. That's why I enjoyed reading. I could stay away from her. Because she had a council house I had my own room. In recent years she would never come in there. If she looked like she was going to try to I would just glare. She would go off then. She knew that I would beat her up – I wanted to."

Kevin felt himself gaping at this outburst. He was discomforted by such intimate revelations.

"Have you ever done something you really regretted? I have quite a lot. Sometimes you hurt only yourself, but other times you hurt other people, sometimes very badly. I have had a lot of time to think recently. I had believed that I was being clever that I was going to become rich and respected - and feared, but I was really just starting down the road my mother had gone. It nearly got me killed."

Kevin found himself drawn to look at her again and the blue eyes flashed back.

"You see Kevin you are not so different we all have our own little hell there just a bit different that's all."

"This rain is terrible. It's been raining for about ten days now there must be some terrible floods."

"There are a lot of floods in low lying land all over the country," said Kevin, grateful to move on to a more neutral topic. "Round Bristol there have been floods up at Gloucester and down in Somerset. Haven't you been watching the news?"

"No, I haven't had a chance to watch TV recently."

"It has been very bad around Manchester with a lot of low lying land flooded."

"God I'm tired!" Ella wound down the driver's window and let the wind and rain blow on her for a few seconds.

"Maybe we should stop somewhere." said Kevin, "I'm afraid that I still don't feel up to driving."

"No!" exclaimed Ella, "I'll wind down the window if I feel bad. In the meantime you can tell me about your life, but make sure that I keep grunting back."

Kevin didn't feel that there was much to tell, but he knew that he had to keep talking to her. So he told her all the humiliations he had suffered at his Bolton school, how he had never had a girlfriend, and his success academically (until now). It was amazing how long it took, and how he would get so absorbed that he would forget to check that she was still listening. However, she seemed genuinely interested and would ask the occasional question.

After joining the M5 at Birmingham he began to run out of steam, but she had got her second wind. She talked a bit then, but mainly about the estate where she lived rather than herself. It sounded very rough. She did say that her former boyfriend had been a drug dealer with pretensions to gangsterhood, and that he had started a local protection racket. She said that, at first, she had been impressed with the authority that he had held on the estate; but that it was how so many people were being hurt that put her off. He had introduced her to cocaine, but she had managed to give it up herself though the withdrawal symptoms had been exceedingly unpleasant.

Kevin was not used to this side of life and he found it disturbing. Fortunately she spared him the details.

Finally they were nearing their destination. They left the M5 at Almondsbury and, after turning down the A38, passed the Aircraft Works at Filton and continued down to Horfield.

Following his directions she turned off the Gloucester Road into a narrow side street and then turned again into an even narrower street, where old terraced houses with flat roofs crowded close to the road. There were cars parked both sides making reverse parking difficult, but fortunately there was a double space just outside Kevin's house and she was able to park easily.

The street light was quite far away and the rain was still lashing down, so there was no one out and about to witness this strange filthy girl entering Kevin's house. She waited on the upstairs landing while Kevin had a pee, and then asked if she could have a shower. She disappeared into the bathroom for about an hour and had a shower and a bath. At her request Kevin passed her in a pair of his pyjamas. She came out then and in the dim hall light Kevin got his first look at her less most of the dirt. She had quite distinctive features. She clearly had African blood with a broad nose and thick lips, but her complexion was very fair with very light brown curly hair, which rose around her head like a misshapen halo. The deep blue eyes though remained the most noticeable feature and they held Kevin in an almost unblinking stare. The dirt must have been thoroughly ingrained because her face and particularly her hands were still very stained.

Kevin showed her to the small guest bedroom (where his mother used to sleep when she visited). She declined a glass of hot milk, but instead excused herself and went straight to bed. The light went off almost immediately.

He went downstairs and into his small living room. He sat for at least ten minutes. He felt that there were things that he should do, but what? Perhaps, he should call the police, but she hadn't done anything except point a toy gun at him, if it was a toy. He felt the panic rising in him again and took some deep breaths. He turned on the TV, to divert his mind from some terrifying fancies. The news was on and, as usual for about the last two weeks, it was mainly about the repeated heavy rain and the very severe and widespread flooding.

It was followed by a comedy quiz programme which lightened Kevin's mood, though by the time he got into bed a cloud had again gathered over him, though this time it was because of the thought of returning to work and having to face Professor Draper.

CHAPTER 2

The light coming through the curtains woke her. She stared at that light. To see it felt like a miracle. It filled her with awe. It could never be mundane again.

She jumped out of bed and pulled the curtains back. She looked out over small gardens backed by a high brick wall and beyond a narrow back lane more tiny gardens and the backs of more houses. Further, beyond the houses quite low in the sky, was a pale watery October sun. The sun! She began to weep with joy, the tears streaming down her face. How she had dreamed of the sun, how she had kept its image sacred in her heart and there it was looking down on her. She was jumping up and down and clasping her hands to her breast like a little girl.

It was about ten minutes before she had calmed down and was able to think again. She had been exceptionally lucky, but only because she had never given up. That last thought brought her back to the strange half-man Kevin. She had meant to leave him there in the road. Two thoughts had made her change her mind. Firstly, it was like abandoning a child. Secondly, there was that image that had constantly come at her out of the dark in the last four weeks, that image of a young man, his eyes glazing over, as he grasped at the mortal gunshot wound in his stomach. Johnny had thought that it was funny, but she didn't, it was a monstrous brutal act in which she had played a part. She had thought that she was hard, that she didn't care, but she had discovered that she did care, very much.

She forced her mind back to Kevin and her present predicament. Had he called the police? She didn't think so. He could have easily left the house leaving the police free to move in. But he knew that she might be armed, perhaps they were bringing in armed police. She controlled herself. If he had there was nothing she could do. She looked out the window again. Along the back lane a smartly dressed woman was leading two equally smart children. They drew opposite the window and carried on; there was no other sign of movement. She breathed a bit more easily. Not the sort of event to occur if the police were out there, believing that they faced a dangerous and desperate armed criminal.

On the dark wooden wardrobe was a full-length mirror. She stared at her own image. Her face was still stained and was covered in scratches and abrasions; it also had a slightly puffy swollen look. The scratches and abrasions were mostly fresh from the last few tumultuous hours, but on her left cheek was an ugly ragged scar, about the size of a two pence coin. She looked at the pyjamas that she was wearing. They were dark cotton pyjamas with a Chinese style pattern. She looked down at her feet. Raw gashes and scrapes stared back. They were clean, but stung sharply.

If Kevin was still here she had to win him over and, since he was a man (probably), the best way to do that was to be as alluring as possible. She undid the top three buttons of the pyjamas to reveal the start of her breasts. She was just thinking that a too ostentatious display would probably make Kevin nervous when something struck her as odd. She stripped of the pyjama top. Her body was also covered in scratches and scrapes, and some slighter older scars along with some remaining ingrained dirt, but what was odd was the size of her breasts. They were definitely larger. Below them her stomach bulged out looking almost swollen and her upper and lower arms bulged. She took of the trousers and looked at her naked body. Her thighs bulged out below her hips and her buttocks looked a lot larger. Last night when washing she had been vaguely conscious of something different, but had been too tired to properly notice. All that fat may have ruined her figure, but it had saved her life. She must have been in that cold water for over an hour and then nearly naked in that wind and rain. She had been cold, but most people would have died.

She put the pyjamas on again, leaving two top buttons undone, and brushed her hair, ineffectually, with the hairbrush lying on the little dressing table. Satisfied, she left the room and went downstairs.

There were two downstairs rooms but they were both very small, the tiny kitchen was out the back and was a simple extension of the hall. The back room had a small dining table with four chairs, and one fireside chair. There was no one in the kitchen or dining room. She went into the tiny front room. It had a small, but comfortable looking dark brown suite, one hard-backed chair, a mantelpiece with a few ornaments, a small TV with a video below it, and in both the recesses created by the chimney breast bookshelves filled with books. Kevin sat on one of the easy chairs.

She looked at him curiously. He had short dark brown, curly hair, a slightly chubby face with a small narrow nose. His body looked soft and rounded. He looked awful. There were bags under his eyes and his complexion was a pasty white. On the small coffee table beside him were a glass of water and three blister packs of paracetamol. The girl's eyes strayed on to them briefly.

"Don't worry!" exclaimed Kevin, "I haven't the courage."

Ella looked at him and smiled.

"Don't be silly!" she scolded gently.

"Have you had breakfast?" she asked. Kevin shook his head.

She kneeled in front of him and took his two hands. Kevin looked miserably into her face.

"I'll cook some breakfast. You'll feel a lot better then."

Cooking breakfast was easier said than done. A small plastic breadbin contained the remains of one mouldy loaf, fit only for the dustbin and in the fridge was a pint of very sour milk. But in the freezer there was one loaf of a sliced brown bread and some sausages. There was also a tin of baked beans, powdered milk and an opened packet of bacon in the fridge that looked edible.

Ella felt completely ravenous and cooked all the passable food. The delicious smell filled the kitchen. She made some coffee and mixed some powdered milk with water. She took two platefuls into the small dining room and called Kevin. He came through slowly and sat down.

"Well!" said Ella, "You get the cutlery, and I'll fetch the coffee."

Once in front of the food, Kevin ate with a reasonable gusto. Ella viewed this with mixed feelings. She was happy to see him eat, but, if he had refused it, she would gladly have eaten his helping as well as her own.

She was just clearing away the plates when the doorbell rang. She looked sharply at Kevin.

"Are you expecting anyone?" She asked.

Kevin shook his head.

"Well, I supposed you had better find out who it is!"

Kevin got up and out into the hall. She heard the door open and voices and, then, a head poked round the dining room door. A pair of brown eyes opened wide in surprise when they caught sight of Ella.

He was about six feet, tanned and muscular and looked as if he was in his mid-thirties. His hair was nearly black, cut short and neat. The face was square, with a small straight nose and full lips that encircled a friendly grin.

"Hullo," he said, "I'm Rich, Richard Murdoch".

As he entered the room his eyes drifted to the carefully arranged pyjama top, which, so far, the self-obsessed Kevin appeared to have completely ignored.

He smiled at her with laughter in his eyes, "Where have you sprung from? Are you another one that Kevin has kidnapped and then stolen their clothes?"

At this remark, poor Kevin who was hovering in the background blushed profusely.

"On the contrary," she smiled back, "Kevin rescued me from those who had. Oh! By the way my name is Ella."

She then gave Rich a highly edited account of what she told Kevin and how he had rescued her.

Rich Murdoch looked at Kevin. "Well, you are a dark horse. I didn't realise that you were a heavily disguised knight in shining armour."

"I am one of Kevin's colleagues," he said, "It would be a great pleasure to chat to you longer Ella, but I am afraid that I am somewhat late and have to rush, but I hope to meet you again. I just like to pop in to visit Kevin, when I'm passing and checking on who he is having breakfast with this time."

Kevin saw him to the door, while Ella stood well back from the window in the front room watching. Suddenly a movement caught her eye. About 50 yards behind Rich was the corner of a side- street and, half-hidden by the corner house a man, his face hidden by a scarf. As Rich turned to move in that direction the figure vanished.

Ella audibly gasped. Could it be the police? Or, even worse, could it be one of Lomax's people?

As Kevin walked in Ella spoke, "Kevin," she said, "Does Rich come here often at the weekend?"

"Yes," said Kevin, "He usually pops in for a few minutes on his way back from shopping at the supermarket."

For the next hour Ella positioned herself to watch that corner, but the muffled figure did not reappear.

As time went on the incident seemed less threatening. Probably, just nerves getting to her.

At some time in that hour Kevin noticed her pyjama top and began to make serious efforts to avoid looking at it.

"Clothes!" blurted Kevin betraying the focus of his attention, "We will need to get you some clothes."

"I will nip up to the supermarket and see if they have any."

"Wait!" said Ella, "I will get you some money."

She went up to her room and dug the battered handbag from under the bed. Inside it, there was a massive wad of very damp five and ten pound notes. Eight hundred pounds, the money for their intended cocaine purchase. She peeled off four fives and two tens, returned the handbag to under the bed and hurried back downstairs.

"Do you have a measuring tape Kevin, I am afraid that I have put on a bit of weight recently."

Somewhat capriciously she asked Kevin to measure her and was highly amused as he blushed uncontrollably as he undertook the task. She wondered how he would get on buying the underwear.

As Kevin was about to leave she suggested that he also get some food and quickly put together a short list. As she watched him go along the very short garden path she had a good look up and down the street, but it was completely empty. She realised that with Kevin gone this would be the time for the police to show their hand. She shut the door and went into the sitting room from where she could again look out of the window on to the street. She stood well back from the window and watched. A man and a woman passed without giving Kevin's house a glance.

After ten minutes had passed she began to relax. Her eyes drifted from the window to the bookshelves. The books were a mixture of textbooks on mathematical topics and more popular books on other science issues. There were also a small number of novels, including crime stories.

She studied the titles of the novels with interest. She liked some romantic novels, but many of them she found annoying. The strong, steadfast, worthy males that the heroines would fall for just did not exist in the real world. Or if they did, she had not met them, only warped surrogates. Johnny had been strong – and crazy. He would have led her to her own destruction and almost did.

It was said that the first romantic novel was 'Jane Eyre'. She had really enjoyed that, as the heroine had been capable of standing up for herself. It was a lesson that she had allowed herself to forget.

Her eyes finally alighted on a battered, paperback version of 'The Secret Garden'. It was a long time since she had read it and she remembered the pleasure it had given her. The young girl of the story was always resourceful and practical, but as the story progresses she also learns to be human. Ella felt that she could identify with her. As it was a children's story, it was also a fairly easy read, which was what she needed at the moment. She picked the book up, opened at the first page and began reading.

The story absorbed her and carried her troubled mind away from her problems. Suddenly, her pleasurable reading was disturbed by the sound of a car in the street and looking up she saw Kevin's small Nova pulling up outside. She was surprised to find that a whole hour had gone by.

For all his shyness Kevin's mission was a complete success and she was soon dressed properly in a pair of elasticated slacks, sweatshirt and a pair of cheap trainers.

"What do you think?"

"OK," mumbled Kevin.

"Come here!" she said, "You deserve a kiss!"

Not waiting she went across to him and planted a kiss firmly on his lips letting it linger for a few seconds.

"There!" she said to a seriously confused Kevin, "You really deserved that. Without you I would still be stuck near-naked and frozen in that awful wood."

She sat down on the sofa and patted the space beside her.

"Come on I won't bite. I need to ask you something."

Kevin sat gingerly beside her.

"Kevin," she started, "I am seriously stuck with nowhere to live and I wonder if I could stay here for a couple of weeks, until I have sorted something out. I would insist on giving you some money for it."

"No problem," mumbled Kevin, insincerely, "The money will not be necessary."

"No, I insist on paying," said Ella, with finality, "And thank you very much. I owe you far more than the money. I would like to give you at least forty pounds a week for the rent and heating and also I will buy some of the food."

Kevin had bought some fresh chicken for tea, but by late afternoon he had become so depressed at the thought of the next day that Ella decided to cook. She roasted it and served it with boiled potatoes and peas from a tin. She found it strange to be preparing normal food again. Kevin's appetite was a lot poorer than at breakfast and Ella ate most of his leftovers.

After tea Ella felt quite vigorous and washed up, since Kevin was making no signs of moving. However, within half-an-hour of finishing she was suddenly hit by an overwhelming tiredness. It was only seven o'clock, but she knew that exhaustion had finally caught up with her.

"I'm sorry Kevin." she apologised, "but I simply have to go to bed."

Kevin, who was sitting slumped in an armchair, made no reply, but she was too tired to notice. She went upstairs washed only her hands and fell into bed.

She awoke in total darkness and, for a moment she thought she was back in the pit. She was sweating and was conscious of rapidly fading, confusing and unpleasant dreams. Had there been a noise? It had probably been part of her dreams. Then she thought that she heard something again. It sounded like a faint sob.

She put on the bedside light. The little alarm clock showed just after two o'clock. She opened the bedroom door and saw that there was a faint light coming from downstairs. She went down. Kevin was still sitting in the living room, where she had left him, but now scattered on the floor around him were at least three empty paracetamol blister packs.

Ella leapt forward, as Kevin turned tearstained eyes towards her. Taking him by surprise she stuck two fingers as far down his throat as they would go. Kevin gagged and vomited up across the living room carpet. The half-digested tea was still vaguely recognisable and scattered amongst it were nearly intact white pills. Dazed Kevin stared at the floor, Ella rushed to the kitchen filled a glass with water and tipped a large amount of cooking salt into it. While stirring it she rushed back to front room.

"Drink this!" she commanded.

Kevin swallowed it down and immediately coughed it back up again. Ella looked at an empty blister pack. It had contained sixteen pills, which, with three blister packs made 48 in all. She sat on her haunches and began to pick out the white pills and fragments from amongst the vomit.

In less than 10 minutes she had sorted them out, 32 intact and 20 fragments, she estimated that there were less than four pills equivalent missing plus some off the softened surfaces.

She looked at Kevin. "I know people who have overdosed on paracetamol - most died slowly and painfully, but one lived crippled and in constant pain. Nothing is worth that!"

She led him upstairs to his bedroom, stripped him to his underwear and got him into bed. Kevin was pliant, but his face was completely grey.

Once he was in bed she climbed into the bed with him. Fortunately, he had a double bed. His body was clammy and cold, but soft almost like a woman. He was neither embarrassed or aroused, so wrapped up was he in his own inner terror. He seemed to be barely aware that she was there.

CHAPTER 3

Kevin opened his eyes. It was morning. His head throbbed and his throat was sore. He remembered what had happened and why. But what had he been thinking, all he had to do was post the letter, he would never have to see Draper again. The bedroom door opened and Ella walked in with a steaming mug. I hope that you like coffee in the morning she said cheerfully, I remembered that you only take milk.

Kevin sat up. "Thank you!" he said, "For saving my life."

"All I have to do is post that letter and I will be free of him."

"Sorry," said Ella, "but I can't allow that."

"What do you mean?" asked Kevin as the terror began to flow back into him. "There is no way I am going to face Draper again."

"It wasn't fear of Draper that made you do what you did last night. It was fear of failure. My advice is to tear that letter up. But at the very least face the man, you will feel much better afterwards."

"I can't!" cried Kevin.

"You won't be alone," replied Ella, "I am coming with you."

"Now drink your coffee, while I make breakfast."

Kevin felt dumbstruck. He seemed to have lost his willpower and he was going to let this woman lead him into disaster. He dreaded the coming clash between her and Draper. Draper would probably have them both thrown off the University campus.

The weather was wet and chilly. The University buildings looked dark and foreboding as Kevin and Ella walked towards them, even though they were low brick buildings of modern construction.

When they had been on the bus, at first, Kevin had thought that Ella looked grim almost annoyed and he had felt her cold blue eyes upon him. This had increased Kevin's misery and terror even more. Suddenly, however, her expression had changed becoming almost distressed and Kevin had thought that her eyes were moist. She had taken his hand then and pressed herself closer to him.

Now as they approached the University buildings she had linked her arm through his and, when he looked at her she would return an encouraging smile. It made Kevin feel better. For the first time since his mother's illness had entered its final stage he did not feel alone.

The Mathematics department consisted of two floors containing lecture halls, seminar rooms and offices. There was also a common room where tea and coffee were served in the mid-morning and mid-afternoon. As they walked through the entrance doorway, the familiar smell of the place hit Kevin. Every building has its own distinctive smell, though some stronger than others, and the smell of the Mathematics building was definitely of the stronger – a mixture of bleach, perfumed cleaning agents and an underlying mustiness from some covert rot. For Kevin it had once been comforting, but now it reminded him of Draper and what he must soon face.

His legs felt like lead. He just wanted to stop. Instead he found himself leading the way to Draper's office.

They passed the porter's box and up the stairs. In the distance, Kevin could hear the loud noise of a lecture hall emptying. The students had been here for a couple of weeks, but Kevin had no lectures scheduled until next term. That had been thanks to Richard Murdoch, who timetabled them, and had taken note of the condition of Kevin's mother.

They passed through a fire door into the first floor corridor. There were now only a few yards left. Ella gripped Kevin tighter as his pace slowed and he grew more rigid. He was finding it increasingly difficult to breathe and was becoming unpleasantly light-headed.

As they got to the door of the outer office it suddenly opened and out came Richard Murdoch. He was dressed in a smartly cut charcoal suit, which contrasted strongly with Kevin's slightly shabby casuals.

"Morning Kevin," Richard said jovially, "Good to see you back in,"

"Not for long," replied Kevin trying to be firm, "I intend to give Professor Draper my resignation."

To this sonorous announcement Richard Murdoch simply laughed.

"You will have to go a long way to give it to him, then," smiled Richard "He's in Houston, Texas at the international conference. He's there for a week and, then, he and his wife are off to Florida for ten days."

Kevin stared. He felt like a man who has just had his execution postponed.

"Somewhat inconvenient time for him to be away." continued Richard, "Jack Sullivan and I have to cover all the lectures."

"Not that I mind, in your case," he added quickly, "Which reminds me."

At this, he assumed a somewhat conspiratorial air.

"Come to my office," he said softly, "You both look as if you could do with a good, strong cup of coffee."

About three doors down from Draper's office, they all turned into Richard's office. He shut the door behind them and offered Kevin and Ella the two battered seats that faced his newer, but flimsy, desk.

The office was about 12 feet square and had once been painted a light yellow, but was now in sore need of a fresh coat. The wall in front of the desk was lined with bookshelves. On these sat battered copies of old mathematical journals, which Kevin knew, had been there since the days of Murdoch's predecessor. The chair behind the desk looked old, but comfortable. To the left of the desk was a small table with some packed lever arch files piled on it, a kettle, a laptop computer, which was on, and a jar of instant coffee. A moderately sized window was to the right of the desk. It looked out over the damp roadway and the neatly trimmed grass of the college grounds beyond.

"Kevin gave you back your clothes, then." said Richard to Ella, as he plugged in the kettle, "It looks like you had quite a rough time," he added more seriously, "There is quite a few nasty cuts on your face and there is still some stains as well."

Ella smiled back at him and said, "The stain above my left eye is a permanent birthmark. The rest should go away and the cuts heal, so I should be soon restored to my natural beauty."

"Kevin, I know that I shouldn't say it but you look pretty bad." Richard observed, "However, I have some more good news for you. In fact, I believe that you could tear up that letter of resignation."

At that point the kettle boiled and Richard took three mugs out of the bottom drawer of his desk along with a small jar of coffee whitener. He prepared the coffees, apologising for the lack of sugar, and passed the steaming mugs round. He then sat back with a rather smug look on his face as he was clearly going to reveal something that he relished.

"You'll never guess," he said, "but Golden Bollocks has fallen from grace. I got the news from Sadie in the office this morning just before meeting you."

For a minute, Kevin felt confused. Who was 'Golden Bollocks'? Then he remembered, it was a term that Richard reserved for Dr Douglas Grant. Dr Grant had arrived from Manchester along with Draper and was clearly an intellectual star. He had proposed a conjecture which is a mathematical statement that is believed to be true, but has not yet been proved. This particular conjecture was not just an academic exercise, since it could revolutionise control software and artificial intelligence, with wide practical application. The conjecture was the main plank of Draper's drive to industry and Grant had been confident of developing its potential much further.

He remembered Grant as a rather dour, but not unpleasant man, who was very much wrapped up in his work. Dr Grant had, however, suffered a terrible tragedy not long before Kevin had left to be with his mother in her last illness. Because of his own problems Kevin had paid little attention, but he knew that Grant's foster-brother had been murdered and that Grant was not taking it well.

"Last Friday Draper gave him a written warning for non-attendance and a low work rate." continued Richard, "And, according to Sadie, he was talking of resigning. He said that there was no point in him continuing here, since his creativity and interest had gone."

Kevin could understand Richard's glee at his colleague's predicament. It took the pressure of both of them.

"I am sorry, but I am a bit lost." said Ella, "How does this affect Kevin?"

"It means," said Kevin, sounding grey and tired, "...that Draper has less reason to get rid of me, since there will now be room for the other man that he is trying to get from Manchester."

"Exactly!" interrupted Richard, "It is also one in the eye for Draper's great project."

"Draper's great project?" Ella asked in puzzlement.

"Our Professor Draper is nothing if not extremely ambitious," answered Richard, "He wants to build up consultancies with some of the country's biggest software houses and process control companies, but he needed Golden Bollock's ideas to give him something to sell."

"A consultancy means that companies pay you lots of money for your ideas," added Richard answering Ella's unspoken question.

"Then won't the failure of Draper's project mean less money coming into the department?" asked Ella perceptively.

"Very true." replied Richard, "Unless someone steps into the breach," he said, looking at Kevin.

"I don't think so." muttered Kevin, who was feeling even more exhausted than before. "I am also sorry for Golden Bollocks, I mean Dr Grant, He seems nice enough and it is not his fault that he is the Professor's favourite."

"Well, I suppose I should have some sympathy for him," replied Richard "but I just can't seem to muster any up."

"I agree with Richard," said Ella, "This is really good news for you Kevin. This morning you thought that you would be walking out of here with no job, and then you find that there is a three week delay and now there is a real opportunity of keeping your job. It just gets better and better."

"I suppose that you are both right," said Kevin, "It increases my chances of keeping my position - and it does mean a great deal to me."

There was a beeping tone and Richard looked at his computer. "Oh hell!" he exclaimed, "I have a lecture in quarter an hour. I suppose I had better read through my notes."

"Yes of course." answered Kevin, getting up. "Thanks for letting me know Rich and good luck with the lecture."

Richard laughed, "I will need it, bloody freshers."

Outside in the corridor, Ella took Kevin's arm and gave it a comforting squeeze.

Kevin led them further down the corridor to an office at the end. On the door in white lettering on a blue panel was printed "Dr Kevin Hansen".

Kevin pushed open the door and he looked around the room. It was nearly as he had left it. An old desk, that surely predated the building, stood with another desk, at right angles to it, on its right hand side. On the second desk rested a computer monitor with a computer tower and behind it a grimy window overlooking a grey scene of wet road and damp parkland. In front of the computer desk was a small table on which sat an ink jet printer. The wall opposite the main desk had a large bookcase up against it, on which were ranked numerous books and folders. Against the wall, opposite the window, were two filing cabinets standing side by side; strewn across the main desk lay a jumble of papers and an open lever arch file. Only an in-tray next to the wall had changed; three or four new journals and one or two letters lay in it.

As he looked around the small cluttered office Kevin realised just how much he wanted this job and how grateful he was. He turned to Ella.

"I owe you so much," he started, "without you I would be dead or worse, but now I have my life and even my job."

Ella smiled.

"Would you like to come home?" she asked, softly, "You look really beat up."

"Not yet," said Kevin, "Having got here I had better make a bit of an effort, but I think that I will leave fairly early."

"See you later, then," said Ella, "I think that it was time that I was going."

She kissed him firmly on the mouth, which left Kevin feeling pleasantly confused.

She had barely left when there came a knock at Kevin's open door. He glanced up and failed to stop the look of surprise that came into his face. Standing there was a young man in his late twenties. His hair was uncombed and his cheeks were sunken. His eyes seemed to pop slightly from their sockets and were bloodshot. His posture was bent and there was a terrible beaten look about him. It took Kevin a few seconds to recognise Dr Douglas Grant. The last time he had seen him, the decline from a well-groomed athletic figure had begun, but now the deterioration had become much worse.

"Dr Grant!" exclaimed Kevin, a little more loudly than he had intended, "Please come in."

"Thank you," said Dr Grant, "I would really like to talk to you."

He sat down and Kevin waited anxiously for him to begin.

"I saw the back of a woman disappearing down the stairs. Did she come from your office?" began Dr Grant rather surprisingly.

"Yes that would have been Ella; a young lady that I met under somewhat dramatic circumstances, but she has done me nothing but good. I was going to resign without even coming in today, but she persuaded me to make an appearance and since then it has... got somewhat better." Kevin finished lamely as he suddenly realised who he was facing.

"Dr Murdoch has been talking to you," smiled Douglas Grant, "But it is no secret. I'm finished!"

He looked thoughtfully at Kevin after saying this and Kevin began to feel embarrassed and started to flush.

"Dr Hansen," he restarted, "I need help and I think that you are the man to give it. There's a lot in it for you."

Kevin gulped.

"As you know Bill Draper has put a lot of faith in me to deliver some radical new ideas, which would put this department on the map. I had got off to a good start. The initial work showed possibilities for both industry and for theoretical advance. I said to him, and I believe it, that there were real opportunities in control systems, artificial intelligence and even evolutionary theory. I was so confident!"

He stopped and for a moment had difficulty continuing. Kevin was worried that the man might actually start to cry.

"All that is now impossible ... for me." he finally continued, "After all that has happened, I intend to go back to Manchester and carry on Mark's work amongst youth. It is the least I can do to pay my debts."

"Mark?" queried Kevin, reluctantly.

"My foster-brother." answered Grant, "You know that he was murdered. Shot by a local hoodlum."

"But would Mark have wanted you to give up your job?" Kevin asked before he could stop the words coming out.

"There are other factors I don't wish to go into." replied Grant, who was now firmly in control of himself.

"The point is I will now be leaving Bill in a hole." continued Grant, "Since it leaves the question of who will carry forward this work."

He then started to answer his own question.

"Bill is a showman, a very intelligent showman, who would be well able to exploit the results, but has neither the patience nor the inclination to do his own research. Jack Sullivan is highly intelligent and capable, but he is not an abstract thinker. As for Richard Murdoch, he does not have the intellect and - quite frankly - is rather lazy."

"That left me with you." Grant added almost theatrically.

Kevin felt that he should interject here, but he was too overwhelmed by his growing awareness of what was coming.

"I read carefully the work that you had done with Professor Thomas on, what was then termed, the New Approach to Chaos theory. It was very good. It was not your fault it didn't lead to anything significant. In fact your work showed that the New Approach was simply not as useful as its proponents had contended."

Douglas Grant paused for a minute and then continued.

"The work that you did with Professor Thomas was the best work that he published. That means that you must have made a significant contribution. I also read through your thesis. There was a lot of good stuff in that as well. You are my one hope Kevin that something of my work will remain. If successful you would become a major name within mathematics and beyond."

For Kevin, this possibility conjured up images of standing before the serried ranks of the mathematical intelligentsia all waiting for his profound words, his mind a blank and him feeling a complete fraud.

"No!" blurted Kevin simply, "It's totally beyond me. You have the wrong man."

Douglas Grant eyed him thoughtfully and let the silence stretch out. Kevin began to feel increasingly uncomfortable and little beads of sweat stood out on his forehead.

"I'm sorry." began Grant, speaking slowly "I have let my enthusiasm carry me away. I believe that Mathematics is an experimental science as much as Physics and Chemistry are. Sometimes one taps into a rich vein and major progress can be made quickly. Other times the ore runs out and initial promise turns to dross ... that will almost certainly happen to my ideas. But Bill needs to know. I do believe that you are the man to follow them through; to show where they run into the sand. And, of course, while doing so you will be in work. I know Bill worries you, but my view is that once he realises he can make no progress here he will move on."

For Kevin, this conjured up a quiet image of working through the theorems deriving from Grant's ideas. It would probably be his last chance to do this sort of work. Work that he was actually good at.

"I suggest," said Douglas Grant, "That I present my ideas to you today. You think about them and make a decision by the end of the week. Unless you have something else planned for today.

"No," said Kevin, "I mean yes your proposal sounds perfectly reasonable, but I am afraid that I have not paid much attention to your work."

"That's alright," replied Douglas, "I will go through it now and I am ready to answer any of your questions."

He stood up and went to Kevin's whiteboard, picking up a dry-marker, and began.

At first, it was as bad as Kevin feared. He had great difficulty following what Grant was talking about and had even more difficulty than normal in maintaining concentration due to his extreme tiredness. After about ten minutes, however, he began to be captured by the excitement and novelty of what Grant was proposing. After twenty minutes he was asking questions and even putting forward very tentative suggestions.

They broke for lunch just long enough to buy sandwiches from the tearoom and immediately returned to Kevin's office to continue working. It was while biting into his not very exciting cheese sandwich that Kevin realised something that turned his interest into real enthusiasm. There was a clear, but far from obvious parallel, in what Douglas Grant was proposing and what he and Professor Thomas had worked through on the New Approach. However, Grant's proposals appeared to have much more potential. He now knew that he could make a contribution.

Over the next hour, it was much more a two way process with Kevin now making significant suggestions. It was starting to come together beautifully. They mapped out a path to turn the original conjecture into a theorem, which meant transforming it from an intelligent guess into a proven mathematical statement. To do it properly though would take much more time, but the hard thinking was done. In the process, other possible connections and propositions began to appear. Kevin found it fascinating. It was so similar to the New Approach, but so much richer in its possibilities. Douglas Grant too was beginning to look distinctly better and his eyes now contained an excited glint.

Suddenly, there was a short knock on the half open door. They both turned and looked. Standing there was a young woman dressed in remarkably smart casual clothes. Her hair though was dishevelled and she looked as though she had just been crying. She was in her early twenties of about average height and slender build. She had straight, pale brown hair hanging to just above her shoulders and a long, oval, pretty face. Her eyes were pale blue and she had a large mouth.

Douglas immediately stood up, his face wearing a mixture of both concern and guilt.

"Karen!" he began, "I'm terribly sorry. I really had to have this discussion with Dr Hansen and I just forgot about our lunch date."

Karen stared at him and a tear began to roll down each cheek.

"It's finished, isn't it?" she said, "I have tried so hard Doug. First I lost Daddy and then after the loss of your brother you have been so distant, so tied up within yourself."

"No!" said Douglas Grant, almost shouting, "It's not over. I admit it, I thought it was, but I do love you. Please accept my apologies. I've been so selfish."

At this Grant moved towards Karen and for a moment she hesitated, almost backed away. Then she moved into his arms and an embrace.

Meanwhile, Kevin sat squirming in his chair not at all sure what to do or where to look.

Finally, Douglas Grant half extricated himself from the gently weeping Karen and turned to Kevin.

"Kevin, thanks so much. The last two hours have restored my sense of purpose, but can we take a break now. I owe Karen at least some of my time. We will start again tomorrow morning if it is OK with you." Kevin mumbled his agreement as they both left.

He stared at the scribblings on his white board. The room was heavy with the smell of the solvent from the dry-marker pens and he walked across to the window and opened it. Outside was a gloomy October afternoon. The leaves on the trees were just starting to change colour, but the earlier heavy rains had already knocked many off and they lay strewn about the grass. Kevin shivered slightly and shut the window.

He pulled out a blank A4 pad and began writing. He felt inspired. At first, it went well and he experienced that wonderful feeling, which was a mixture of both excitement and satisfaction, as the logic carried him on. However, after about one hour he began to flag and the clarity began to fade.

He sat back in his chair. He felt very tired. The last three hours had been such a mental roller coaster, he had not noticed how exhausted he was. He tried not to think of the awesome responsibilities that Dr Grant was thrusting on him. He looked at his wall clock. It was already after four o'clock. The day had flown by, but then it had been quite a late start.

For some reason he thought of Karen and that made him think of her father. The late Sir George Reading had been both a ruthless businessman and well-known philanthropist. There were indeed many that said that the sole reason for his philanthropy had been to obtain his knighthood. Whatever the truth, it had been of great benefit to the University. The combined staff club and gymnasium was called the Sir George Reading House after him, because he had financed it. There had also been many other generous donations to the University, which had supported it against the constant belt-tightening of local and central government.

There had been though another side to the late Sir George. Several years ago he had been arrested for soliciting in the Kings Cross area of London and there were stories of wild parties. His treatment of those who had worked for him had been both highly exploitative and brutal. There was no doubt, however, that he had loved his only daughter and been surprisingly close to her. Her mother had died having a second child, who had also not survived. Karen, in turn, loved him. He had died suddenly about three months ago of a heart attack. Karen had been terribly upset.

She had been going out with Douglas Grant at the time and he had been supporting her well until his own tragedy had struck.

Kevin shook himself. His musing had almost drifted into sleep. He had to get home. He turned off the office light and shut the door. At the bottom of the stairs by the porter's box he could still hear voices coming from the tearoom that was on the ground floor corridor. As he looked in that direction Douglas and Karen came through the double fire door. Douglas looked grim and Karen had gone very pale, but they were still arm in arm and to Kevin looked even closer and more of a couple than he had ever seen before. They passed him nodding briefly and left the building. Kevin loitered at the notice board pretending to be engrossed in a poster about a student gardening club, but actually allowing them to get well clear. He did not think that this would be an appropriate time to be with them.

CHAPTER 4

The "Blue Bird" cafeteria in the Ashbury's supermarket had looked bright and inviting and Ella had decided to have a cup of coffee. It was just after three o'clock and Ella was sitting back having been on her feet for most of the day. However, she was finding it impossible to relax. She was concerned that she might have made a very serious mistake. She thought back over her day.

After having left Kevin at the University in the late morning she had decided to walk back to his house. She felt a tremendous urge to be outside. The outside was something she now valued very strongly. Even though it was a gloomy and damp day, it still felt wonderful to her. In addition, the small rooms in Kevin's house gave her a shut-in feeling, which was uncomfortably close to how she had felt when she had been trapped.

She was walking along a pedestrian path next to the dual carriageway for about ten minute when she had noticed the large Ashbury's supermarket to her right. She went in initially to buy some extra food for the meal that night, but had immediately spotted the prominent adverts for jobs. Although she was very keen on getting some sort of work, she didn't feel very confident yet. Her face was still fairly battered and stained and would need to be explained and could raise suspicions. She had a National Insurance number in the name of Ella Slater, but she wasn't sure that it would be adequate and that it would not expose her. Still, there seemed no harm in asking for a job application, which was readily available at the customer service desk. The young girl behind the desk cheerfully told her that she could have an interview that afternoon, if she wanted.

Ella thought about it as she had walked down Gloucester Road. If she was in employment it was another step to re-inventing herself. She liked that term "re-inventing". It was a word that she had picked up from a book about a criminal, who had become a respectable citizen with a new name and associates. It was an ideal model for what she intended to do.

She dropped off the food, which she had bought, at Kevin's house and carried on down Gloucester Road. There was something old-fashioned about Gloucester Road. It was a single carriageway road, which led down to the centre of Bristol. Small residential streets led off each side. The buildings were generally quite old, most predating the Second World War. Gloucester Road itself was lined with small shops, interspersed with old pubs, some labouring under modernised names. Even on a Monday afternoon the pavements were busy with shoppers.

Ella found it fascinating. It was so different from the estate where she had lived with its row upon row of sixties semi-detacheds and maisonettes and the occasional shopping centre with its shuttered, dead shops.

As she wandered down Gloucester Road she had gone into several charity shops. She was amazed at the value she could obtain there and, with care, she had been able to buy herself some smart clothes. Shoes had been trickier. She had had to buy them new. She eventually settled for a pair of flat shoes for everyday wear and a pair of high heels with a somewhat lower height than the current fashion demanded. They made her feel more comfortable and also they were less ostentatious. Unlike the clothes, they had knocked a significant hole into her money reserve.

She caught a bus back up Gloucester Road and returned to Kevin's house. She, then, dressed in a white blouse and dark-blue skirt with a matching jacket. The effect was of understated smartness. As she looked at herself in the mirror she felt her confidence growing and decided that she would try for the job. She ate a couple of cheese sandwiches and then considered the problem of references. She plumped for the names of a teacher and the headmaster at her old school. The real Ella Slater had been quite successful at school, her disintegration had come later. She had felt a pang then as she thought about the fate of the woman whose identity she now wore.

The interview at Ashbury's was conducted by a friendly middle-aged woman. She had been sympathetic to Ella's story of a recent motor bike accident and how she had been unable to do much work since school as she had had to look after her younger brothers and sisters, following the death of her mother. Ella had practised the stories before coming and had nearly convinced herself of their reality. The woman was particularly impressed with Ella's knowledge of meats and butchering. It was the one job that she had really had. It had lasted six months and she had learned well. The butcher's shop had then shut down, like so many other shops on the estate, and Ella's experience of regular employment had come to an end. The woman finished interviewing by saying that Ella would be phoned within the next two days.

Ella had, initially, felt very pleased with her performance, but now as she sat in the cafe reflecting on the implications she felt increasingly nervous. Would they check the references? Would "irregularities" show up with the Inland Revenue? With an effort she checked the rising panic. It was a move that she had to make and better sooner than later.

Outside Ashbury's she had to wait nearly twenty minutes for a bus, which was a small, short, single-decker. As she slumped into a seat, she began to feel a tiredness overwhelm her. With the tiredness came doubts, fears and guilt. What she was trying to do seemed suddenly too much. What she had done to survive seemed beyond redemption.

She was glad to reach Kevin's house. She was surprised to find that Kevin was not yet home, as it was well after four o'clock. Earlier the house had seemed too small almost suffocating. Now she was glad of its size. It seemed to surround her like a protective shell. The outside had suddenly become too large. She sat down on the couch in the sitting room and leaned back. Her eyes closed.

Kevin looked at his watch. It was just before five o'clock. Although, earlier he had been dead tired, he now felt strangely elated. The excitement of the session with Douglas Grant, the reawakening of old dreams, the possibility of doing new, exciting work. He thought of Ella then. He owed her a great deal. Without her, at best, he would have been unemployed at worst he would have been dead.

He reached his own front door and went in. From the hall he could see Ella curled up on the sofa. She looked smaller than he remembered. Her deep breathing revealed that she was sound asleep. He looked at her closely, curiously. The piercing blue eyes, which so disconcerted him, were hidden beneath closed lids. Her very fair, tightly curled hair sprayed about her head in its inevitable disorder. For the rest, though, she was dressed smartly in a dark blue jacket and skirt with a white blouse. Kevin found his eyes lingering on her exposed stockinged thigh. He dragged them away in some confusion and looked at her face. It was a strange, fascinating face. It was very fair with freckles, but had the features and contours of an African face. It was far from graceful; it was broad with a large, but flat nose and full lips. Above the left eye a brown mark stood out. At first Kevin thought that it was a stain, like some of the other fainter marks. Then he remembered that she had said that she had a birthmark there. She was slightly plump with a bulge at her stomach and heavy thighs.

Kevin felt that he was being rude and started to feel embarrassed. He quietly left and went into the kitchen. He checked in the freezer and found two readymade pizzas that he presumed Ella had bought. They were ideal, as he did not feel like cooking. He did them one after the other in the microwave, keeping them warm in the cooker oven. The delicious smell of oregano and hot cheese filled the kitchen and Kevin realised how hungry he was.

"What's cooking?" sounded a sleepy voice from the other room.

"The pizzas," answered Kevin, "and they're nearly ready."

He cut the pizzas into slices and put them on to two plates. Ella looked up as he brought them through.

"If you don't mind, we may as well eat them in here."

"Suits me," replied Ella, "I don't feel like moving."

He sat down beside her and passed her a plate loaded with pizza slices. She leaned against him and Kevin felt the warmth and softness of her body. The feeling of elation was still with him and he felt curiously detached. Normally, a woman this close would disturb him, but instead it just felt pleasant.

Between mouthfuls of pizza, he told Ella what had happened after she had left the university. The temptation to get carried away with the mathematics was almost irresistible, but he managed to keep it to the essentials. Finally, Ella looked up into his face.

"Kevin that's wonderful." she said, "Surely, this means that your job is secure."

"Very likely," answered Kevin "and it means that I will really be achieving something, as well."

Ella wiped the crumbs from around her mouth. She bent her head up to his and pulled him towards her and kissed him firmly. Kevin felt both anxious and happy at the same time. He did not know how to proceed and felt sure that he would disappoint.

"Don't worry," said Ella, softly, seeming to sense his mood, "Just hold me. It's what I need."

He held her and she kissed him again and nibbled at his ears.

She spoke to him quietly, then, the tone meaning more than the words.

"Kevin, touch me, don't let me go."

For several minutes, they kissed and caressed each other. Kevin felt an air of unreality surround him. He could not believe that it was happening. His hands moved over her body, seemingly by their own volition. Her softness was exciting. Her need was exciting.

"Come!" she exclaimed finally, "I want you in bed."

Kevin was led upstairs. His normal anxiety was muted by that feeling of detachment brought on by exhaustion and also a pleasurable feeling of anticipation. In the unlit bedroom, Ella stripped off his clothes and hers alternatively.

"Come to bed," she whispered as she gently pulled him into bed after her.

As they clung together in the bed Kevin was conscious of his arousal against her body and a feeling of acute embarrassment passed over him. He also felt a tremendous desire to hold her. It wasn't that he was at last having an opportunity to be with a woman, it was that he felt a deep love for her, which he quietly told her. She pulled him on top then and guided him in. She moaned under him and Kevin felt his excitement rising and his body reacting. She responded in turn and his excitement rose again. Finally, a great wave passed through him and their bodies shuddered and arched together.

Afterwards they spoke the sweet words of their love and then both fell asleep.

When Ella awoke it was still dark, but in the distance she could hear a milk float trundling about its business. The soft body beside her felt warm and she enjoyed its comforting presence. She had, of course, been intending to seduce Kevin for a while, but she had been surprised how much she actually needed him. The question of his potency had worried her a bit and she had even bought some 'aids' from a shop on the Gloucester Road, but had Kevin had a problem she would not have used them last night. She would simply have held him and told him not to worry.

In fact, despite his obvious virginity, it had been Kevin who had surprised her. All her earlier lovers had been better endowed, more inventive and more vigorous than Kevin, but for all the affection, concern and love that they had shown her they might as well have been stray dogs. Making love to Kevin had satisfied her in a way that none of the rest had got near to doing. He had touched her heart.

Her confidence had come back. It had been odd yesterday how her confidence had ebbed and insecurity had got the better of her. The job at Ashbury's was a risk, but she was used to taking risks. Even if something did go wrong, the most likely thing to happen was that she simply would not keep the job. Also, she had had this desperate need for the protecting comfort of Kevin's arms. It had been pleasant in a new and revealing way, but why the desperation.

The growing discomfort from her bladder became impossible to ignore. She would have to go to the toilet.

It was there that she found the answer. On the toilet paper she had used to dry herself were the revealing pink spots. Her period had started. She thought of where she had been when she had had her last one. No wonder she had forgotten that it was due.

Last night, she had been careless. They had used no birth control or any protective. Well she did not think that a woman was fertile just before her period. Nor did she think that she was likely to catch anything from Kevin, though the reverse situation was far less certain. She had better start marking the calendar. This was clearly a time when she was most likely to make mistakes.

Kevin stirred and she immediately cuddled up close to him. It was very pleasant how comforting he was. It would be true to say that he was her first real lover.

CHAPTER 5

Douglas Grant was speaking, but Kevin was finding it very hard to concentrate on the words. His mind was still in bed with Ella. The feel of her soft warm body still echoed through his senses. In the morning, she had taken his hand and guided it gently round her body. In the darkness, Kevin had felt his embarrassment much less. There was something intimate and private about touch, which light would have dispersed. The tour had been exciting and complete. She took him to every part, told him softly what to caress and how to caress it. The feel of the moist warmth at the centre of her womanhood had aroused him so much that they had made love again.

"Kevin, are you listening to me? I feel like I am talking to myself," said Douglas Grant interrupting his own preamble.

Douglas Grant fought to control himself. He knew from yesterday that Kevin was a slow starter, but once his mind got into gear he was truly brilliant and his logic was remorseless. However, usually Kevin wore an anxious and worried look as he struggled to get to grips with what was being said, but, today, he just sat there, a faint smile on his face, clearly not even trying.

Douglas tried again not to get angry. He too was different from yesterday. After his session with Kevin he had felt encouraged and strong enough to make his confession to Karen. She had been visibly shocked and horrified, but she had held his hand and pulled him close. He had felt deeply comforted by her support, but he knew that she could not agree with what he had done. After all, he could not support it. It had been an appalling crime, which had resulted in the terrible deaths of three people. True those people were not innocent. Two had carried out the murder of his dear foster brother, Mark, and the other was helping destroy young lives with drugs. He had called them the gangster, the slag and the thug. The first two names had come first and the last after the event. He knew what he was trying to do, dehumanise your enemy. It had not worked. Whatever they were or had done, they were now dead people and he had killed them, just as much as if he had pulled the triggers of the guns himself.

Karen's response had been unequivocal. He must go to the police. A serious and brutal crime had been committed and he had been a witness to it. She did not understand why he delayed. This was why he was so annoyed by Kevin's lack of concentration. Once he had confessed to the police, then there would be a court case against the perpetrators and he would be the key witness. These people were major criminals and he would probably have to go into hiding. There may even be charges against him. Before this happened, he had to ensure that the work continued. He badly needed Kevin for this. No one else was remotely capable.

He thought back to his father. He had been a leading gangster and hard man on the estate over a decade earlier. From what his few relatives had said his mother had been totally the opposite. She had been a kind and considerate woman. She had died not long after he was born. At first, he had been looked after by an aunt, who was actually his true uncle's ex-wife. Her life though had been becoming increasingly chaotic and, after two years, he was fostered by the Ashton family, where he stayed until he left Manchester to come to Bristol with Bill Draper.

He had seen his father several times before he was twelve, when his father was charged with armed robbery and died shortly afterwards while on remand. Not long before that, he had had his last meeting with his father. He had been a short, squat, muscular man with close cut hair, a square head, thin lips and hard unsympathetic eyes. Those eyes had locked on to him, appraising him.

"You're so like your mother." he had said, "Sensitive and soft. Whatever you do, don't try and be like me. You could never take the heat."

At the time, he had thought that his father had just been stating his disappointment in his son; but he now knew, too late, that the words had been both profound and shown true insight.

He had actually thought after Mark's murder and the lackadaisical police response, "What would dad have done in this situation?"

The answer had been clear, "Get even!"

He had got even and the bitter taste of vengeance was choking the life out of him.

He, suddenly, became aware again of Kevin, who was still muttering an embarrassed apology.

"Let's break for an early tea." Grant sighed.

Despite the inauspicious start the rest of the day went very well. In the afternoon, they even managed to complete a full proof, which, although fairly straightforward, was critical to the rest of the work. It was just after five when they decided to call a halt. Both were pleased and happy with their day's work.

It was about half past five and Ella was dragging herself about the kitchen trying to prepare a meal. Her period was in full flow and, although the feeling of depression and doubts had gone, she felt completely drained of energy. She had not strayed far from the house that day, except to look at some of the second hand shops on Gloucester Road again, but she had only bought a pair of leggings. The walk though had done her good and eased the period pains. In the afternoon, a woman from Ashbury's had phoned to tell her that she had got the job and that they would like her to start on Thursday for an early morning shift. This had pleased Ella. By tomorrow she would be feeling a lot better and by Thursday she would be almost her normal self.

She heard the front door opening and closing. She walked out into the hall to greet Kevin. One look at his face told her that he had had another good day. He had a far-away look in his eyes, but also an air of vitality that was usually lacking. She had just the job for him.

While Kevin prepared fish fingers, instant potatoes and peas, Ella took her shoes off and put her feet up on the couch. She reflected on her current situation. What did she think of Kevin? He was so different from what she was used to. He was weak and depressive and of a type that only a short time ago she would have despised. There was no doubt though that she both cared for him and, more surprisingly, needed him. His gentleness and, almost female, softness were reassuring. There was no threat from him, no attempt to impose his will, no violence. She needed a non-violent man. Not so much because of the physical harm that a violent man would do to her, but what they led her to be part of. In her mind's eye she could still see the young man that she had helped kill.

She got up of the couch, padded through into the kitchen in her stockinged feet. Kevin was busy frying four fish fingers in a small frying pan. She tapped him on the shoulder and when he turned round kissed him firmly on the mouth and held him in an embrace.

"That's because I love you," she said to a dazed Kevin as she returned to her position on the couch. Meanwhile, Kevin turned back to his rapidly darkening fish fingers.

CHAPTER 6

Three o'clock on Thursday afternoon found Ella again in the Blue Bird cafe enjoying a cup of tea. This time she was not alone. She was chatting with a stocky youth with short blond hair and a very young looking girl. Ella and the girl had both started working in Ashbury's that day, while the youth had been working there for a year. The young man spoke with the air of one who had had a lifetime of experience. His attention was mainly directed to the young girl who had a pretty, small-featured face and blond hair. Ella was 21 and must have appeared ancient to him. Ella was enjoying the company, but the young man did seem to be creating a favourable impression with the girl, so Ella felt that she should make her excuses and go.

"Sorry, but I've got to rush, I'll see you both bright and early tomorrow," she said cheerfully.

"Not so bright," responded the young man, ruefully.

Outside the overcast gloom of the last two days had cleared and the day was one of those pleasant, clear autumn days with a hint of winter chill. Ella walked the few yards to where the bus stopped. The bus came right into the Ashbury's car park. As usual for three o'clock midweek, this end of the car park was full and even the end furthest from the entrance was reasonably well filled.

Waiting for the bus she reflected on what had been a relatively successful morning. It had been so long since she had worked, she had worried that she might not cope. In fact it went very well and she had impressed her supervisor with her knowledge of different meats and cuts.

The autumn sun shone weakly and with little warmth, but Ella found that it filled her with a feeling of elation. Only one week ago, she was trapped in the dark and had almost forgotten what the sun had looked like. She reflected on how well she had survived it and how healthy she felt. She had, of course, eaten well. She had remembered reading that lean meat on its own was poisonous due to high nitrogen levels attacking the kidneys. Therefore, if one lived on animal protein, one should eat large amounts of the fat. This was how the Eskimos survived. The fat had resulted in her putting on weight, but had protected her from the intense cold. It was strange how such terrifying events were already becoming distant, almost as if they had never happened.

She thought again of Kevin. He was clearly having a good week. The work with this Dr Grant seemed to be going very well. She was always suspicious and she wondered if Dr Grant would simply use Kevin and claim Kevin's ideas as his own. He sounded a lot worldlier than Kevin. However, he probably would not, as from what Kevin said, Grant seemed to be still obsessed with the death of his brother. She deliberately moved her thoughts on. She did not like to think of young men dying violently.

Could she live with Kevin for a long time? It could get boring after a while, but at present she enjoyed the peace. Nor was she the type of girl who was desperate to get out. Not now that she was not living in her mother's house.

She thought then of her mother, of her obesity, of her total corruption. She was so happy to be far away from her. Her mother had originally come from Ireland and had had flaming red hair when she was young. It had now turned grey, but her mother kept it dyed an artificial looking red. She would sit on her couch eating chocolates and watching TV all day. Now that her professional life was finished no one came to visit her. With Ella gone, she could die in her chair and it would be unlikely that anyone would notice for weeks.

The bus arrived too soon, as Ella was still enjoying the sun. The journey back was pleasant though as she gazed out at the sunlit houses. Such simple things could now give her so much pleasure.

The bus was nearly at her stop and had just turned into Gloucester Road from Filton Avenue when she saw a familiar figure walking up Gloucester Road. It was Richard Murdoch.

"What on earth was he doing there at this time of day?" she thought.

Then she remembered that University lecturers were not like normal wage slaves and were much freer to come and go. He was probably shopping, though most of the shops were further down Gloucester Road. The half-formed observations left her mind as she got off the bus.

Ella decided that that night she would have a go at cooking a proper meal. On Tuesday, she had just been too tired and last night she had felt a bit grumpy. Poor Kevin, she had upset him a bit. She would make amends.

After a brief lunch of sandwiches, she again went down Gloucester Road to have another look in the charity shops. She was after a dress that she could wear that evening. She found a low cut one that was ideal and would give Kevin an eyeful. It was maroon with dainty white frills. She also found another dress that was a bit more staid, but could be very useful if she and Kevin went out. Both were ridiculously cheap. She returned to Kevin's house with her booty and immediately went back out again to a local Somerfield's, which was nearby on Gloucester Road.

There she bought some chicken, cook in the bag basmati rice, a tin of a white wine sauce and a bottle of real white wine. She also bought some broccoli to go with the meal. She was really quite enjoying herself.

Back at Kevin's, she got to work. She casseroled the chicken with the wine sauce, prepared the broccoli for cooking in the microwave and placed a pan of water on the cooker ready to boil. She then went through to the small back dining room. She found a new tablecloth and some stylish, deep red, paper serviettes. On the table, she placed two dumpy pink candles with matching glass bases that she had just bought. She set the two places and put out two matching wineglasses that she had found. She turned off the main light, leaving only a small table lamp on. With the candles lit the effect should be just right.

Just after that she had one bad moment. Her mind had wandered back to Johnny Masters. She had had this fantasy view of him, in which he was this leading gangster figure and she was his girl. It was not just that Johnny had led her astray and she had played a passive, masochistic role, but that she had positively encouraged him. For a moment, she had a feeling of irredeemable guilt and she felt like giving up her plans for the evening. Then the iron in her soul reasserted itself. What was done was done, she had been lucky to survive and she had to move on.

Kevin returned at about half five. He was in high spirits and had clearly had another good day. She suggested that he should go upstairs and shower and change, while she finished off the meal. When he came down again the meal was ready and she had changed into the rather daring dress. She was pleased, in a capricious way, to see his discomfort as he tried to keep his eyes off her front.

"Look as much as you like," she laughed, "I put it on for you, but don't touch until after the meal. I don't want to starve."

She playfully grabbed his face between her two hands and forced him to look.

"There!" she giggled, "Now let's eat."

Over the food, they chatted freely about how Kevin's work was going and how Ella liked Bristol or, at least, the Gloucester Road part that she had explored. For Ella, the only bad moment was when Kevin mentioned the murder of Douglas Grant's brother. It reminded Ella of that other young man. He, too, had had a family who would mourn his loss and lament the waste of a young life. She had looked at Kevin then straight in the eye and had told him that she loved him exactly as he was.

The food, a little wine and the intimate conversation led them into the bedroom, where they made love, chatted and made love again. Neither was as tired as they had been on their first night and it was quite late by the time that they finally fell asleep in each other's arms.

CHAPTER 7

It was Sunday, and the late afternoon sun was sinking down over the coast to Ella's right, while straight ahead stretched the endless mud of Weston-Super-Mare. The breeze off the sea was growing chill, but it did not trouble Ella. It had been the perfect end to a perfect week. They had come down to Weston early in the morning arriving just after nine o'clock. The day had been beautifully clear and sunny and Ella was slightly afraid that she might even have got sunburn. Her face was already starting to feel as if it was glowing.

Kevin had gone to fetch fish and chips and Ella was enjoying those last moments on the beach.

"Could it last?" she asked herself.

She was beginning to feel more confident that she was going to get away with it. Lomax had almost certainly leaked the word that she and the others were dead, as a deterrent to discourage anyone else from cheating him.

The main problem was if the bodies were discovered. The condition of Tulley's remains would raise a lot of questions. But who would want to go down that shaft. The water level had never quite got to the top of the shaft and the last she had seen of Johnny's decomposed body was it bobbing up and down on the water about five feet below. The longer those remains were undiscovered the less that could be learned from them. She definitely felt that she could start to relax.

Her relationship with Kevin had rapidly developed an intensity that had been totally unexpected, but she could not tell him the truth. If he were to find out it would be over. She could imagine that he would just retreat back into his shell, seeing their love as simply another misfortune thrown at him by life.

Kevin returned with the fish and chips and they sat close together on the bench looking out over the endless mud to the distant sea.

"Why is there so much mud?" she asked puzzled.

"Because," replied Kevin, "Both up the coast and down the coast are two long peninsulas of hard rock sticking about a mile out to sea. The mud is carried down from the rivers further up the Severn estuary, but when it reaches here the water is trapped in the inlet and stops moving and, thus, drops its load of mud. It's a process that's being going on for over ten thousand years, since the last ice age. The result is an awful lot of mud, which you can now see before you."

As he finished, he waved with a flourish towards the mud. Ella looked out over it. In the gathering gloom, it was almost black. It made her shiver uneasily. She was glad when they got up to return to the car.

Ella sat back comfortably in the passenger seat. It was really time that she sat her test and got her license. On the journey down, she had found Kevin's non-positive driving extremely irritating. He drove extremely slowly at only fifty miles per hour and was very nervous of other traffic. On the few occasions that there was a vehicle going slower than they were, he would pull out about a quarter mile early. At junctions he would wait for the road to be totally clear before pulling out much to the obvious annoyance of cars waiting behind him.

Now on the return journey, Ella was feeling so relaxed and contented that not even Kevin's driving could get to her. She was feeling confident that the re-invention of herself was going to work. She was successfully in work. She had an eccentric, but strangely comforting, lover. She had a place to stay. Most of all she was still alive and free.

She considered her sanity for a moment. What she had gone through could have driven others mad. However, she had tackled each problem as it came along, never trying to look too far ahead. There were some nightmares, but they were manageable. There was only one image that deeply disturbed her. It was not the cutting of decaying human flesh, the sight of Tulley's hollow, decapitated, dismembered carcass or of Johnny's dead black eyes. Even the thought of dying trapped in that pit lay peaceful in the past. What haunted her mind and ambushed her peace was a young man staggering back with a dazed look in his eyes a mortal bullet wound in his stomach. She looked, lovingly at Kevin then. That was why she needed him.

The day at Weston had reinvigorated her and the autumn sun had been strong enough for her face to now be glowing. They were coming down the A38 having left the M5 at the Almondsbury interchange. It was completely dark now. As she lay back the orange-yellow of the sodium streetlights flashed overhead. She sat up and looked out of the window; they had just about reached the turn-off on that led to Kevin's street. She thought fondly of the comfort of Kevin's small house. Her sense of well-being increased.

After his usual delay, Kevin turned right of Gloucester Road. Ella jerked fully awake. Straight-ahead just beyond the junction to Kevin's street a police car was parked in the middle of the road its headlights on and its blue lights flashing. A policeman moved out into the street signalling Kevin to halt. Ella felt herself close to panic, her dreams of the last hour disintegrating.

As Kevin stopped the car, the policeman signalled him to pull into the side. Kevin did so and the policeman walked towards them and tapped on Kevin's window. Beads of sweat developed on Ella's forehead and her stomach churned. Kevin and the policeman looked distant and unreal like actors in a play. Kevin's face wore the look of mild concern characteristic of an innocent citizen. The young policeman, who at any moment was going to arrest Ella, wore an expression of almost boredom.

Kevin wound down the window. The policeman looked casually into the car his eyes stopping at both Kevin and Ella.

"Sorry, to inconvenience you, sir, but we're just about to bring an ambulance down the street and it's so narrow that we have to keep it clear."

At that moment the police car ahead suddenly leapt into life and raced passed them, its siren sounding. Immediately, turning from the street just up from Kevin's an ambulance appeared and roared off in the wake of the police car.

"OK sir, you can go on now."

"Thanks officer," replied Kevin.

"That was strange," said Kevin, as he finished parking the car, "I don't think that they normally give an ambulance a police escort. Something serious must have happened."

"It gave me a bit of a fright," replied Ella, unguardedly, "I thought that they were going to stop you for speeding." she added weakly, trying to cover up.

"Was I going too fast?" asked Kevin in a serious tone, the irony lost on him.

Ella laughed and reached across to give him a kiss.

CHAPTER 8

Kevin got off the bus and walked the short distance across the University campus to the mathematics building. It was only eight o'clock, but the sun was already up and clearing the heavy dew. He and Douglas Grant had agreed on Friday to get an early start this Monday morning and try and make significant progress today. It was no sacrifice for him, because he had got up with Ella before six, as she was starting work at seven.

He let his mind linger on Ella. It was hard to believe that they had only been together for just over a week. At first, he had been so afraid and suspicious of her. He had just wished that she would go away. She had been good for him from the beginning. If she hadn't pushed herself into his life, he would have spent a miserable night at the roadside. He would have no job; he could even be dead by his own hand. Now it was all working out so well. Not only did he have a job, but also it was going particularly well. It could all change when Draper came back, but Draper no longer terrified him.

He thought then about her. She had undoubtedly had a very harsh and loveless upbringing. There was a hardness in her and a will to survive that frightened him. There was also though a great need for gentleness and love, which he found himself responding to. He loved her. What surprised him was that she loved him for what he was. Most women found his lack of confidence and irresolution a complete turn off. Only once many years ago had a particularly motherly woman shown an interest in him, but there had only been room for one mother in his life.

There was nothing motherly in the way Ella treated him. She loved him as a man. In turn, she made him respond like a man, he felt both loving and protective towards her. That last emotion, he found particularly odd. She seemed so resilient and self-contained. Somewhere a dissident voice in

43

his head pointed out that he should be asking questions about her. He knew why he did not. He was too happy with the present situation and had an uneasy feeling that it was fragile.

He entered the mathematics department and noticed that the familiar smell felt comforting again, as it had done when Professor Thomas had been in charge. His office was still empty, when he entered it. Dr Grant had not yet arrived. He put a little blow heater on as the central heating had only just come on and the radiator under his window was just starting to warm up. He then went to the staff toilet just along the corridor to fill the kettle and then returned to his office and plugged it in.

It was just boiling as, with impeccable timing, Douglas Grant arrived. As he walked in, Kevin looked up at him and thought how much better he was looking than one week ago. He was walking erect and his natural colour had returned. Ella had been good for him as well. If it had not been for her, there would have been no Kevin to be there for Douglas to share his work with and his descent would have continued.

"Good man!" exclaimed Douglas, eyeing the boiling kettle "I really need a cup of coffee."

"How's Karen?" asked Kevin a little cautiously.

"She fine." answered Douglas, "Thanks to you, this past week has really lifted my spirits. Before that, I was treating her so badly."

"Thank Ella," responded Kevin, "If it had not been for her, I would not be here. In fact, I would probably be dead."

He then explained to Douglas how Ella had saved his life.

"Here's to Ella, then," said Douglas raising his steaming mug to his mouth "It's time that I met this amazing woman of yours."

The first hour passed quickly, as they laboured over a proof. They had completed it and were beginning to discuss the further implications when there came a knock at the door and they turned to see a trim, slender woman, in her early thirties standing at the partially open door.

She bore with her an air of ordered efficiency and her appearance reflected this. A smart, white blouse, partly covered with a pale brown, mock waistcoat, fitted neatly over her narrow shoulders and small breasts. A nearly matching pale brown, skirt fitted round her slender waist and down to her knees.

"Come in, Sadie," said Douglas Grant, responding first, "What can we do for you?"

"I am sorry to interrupt," she replied, "But I have just had a phone call from Richard Murdoch. He says that he is feeling really unwell and won't be able to come in today. He was hoping that Dr Hansen could take his fresher class, since he did the same course last year."

"Impossible!" retorted Douglas, almost shouting, before Kevin could collect his thoughts, "The class will just have to be postponed and Dr

Murdoch will have to arrange an extra session."

Sadie, however, held her ground. "Well!" she responded, "I would have thought that of all people you two could have been more cooperative, as I know that Dr Murdoch went to a lot of trouble to cover the lectures for the whole of this term when the pair of you couldn't manage them."

Kevin felt himself reddening. Sadie was right, Richard had indeed gone to a lot of trouble to cover up for them both and Douglas' response had sounded particularly churlish, probably, reflecting the always present animosity between him and Richard.

He sighed and Douglas glared at him. "Sadie's right Douglas, Richard has done a lot to cover for us."

"What time is this lecture?" Kevin then asked Sadie.

"I am afraid that it is in a half-hour at 10 o'clock."

Kevin heart sank and he felt an anxiety creep over him. He had the notes in one of the lever arch files, which sat in his bookshelf.

"Do you know, which topic it was to be today," he queried.

"He said that he was going to do methods of integration."

Kevin felt some relief. It was a topic that fascinated him and, therefore, one where he was confident of his own knowledge.

He looked back at Douglas.

"OK," said Dr Grant, resignedly, "I suppose we have got to a point, where I could explore some of the possibilities myself ... and good luck."

Kevin entered the lecture room. It was the biggest lecture room in the building and the one that he hated most. He always associated it with teaching freshers. The room was typical of the 1970's with a lecture platform with rows of benches sloping up away from it, but at a much shallower angle than the lecture rooms of an earlier generation. The benches still had a slightly modern air to them, but were becoming distinctly tatty.

Freshers were the main problem. Fresher audiences consisted of a lethal mix of young people who had just been released from the confines of school intermingled with those repeating their first year. This latter group, though relatively small in numbers, were the worst. They would be even worse this year as many of them remembered the fun they had had at his expense the previous year.

It was true. His entrance was accompanied by a roar that grew louder as the new entrants began to realise that there was fun to be had here. The situation was made worse by having to struggle with the microphone and then finding that the amplifier did not work.

"What had Richard said? Speak as if you were talking to someone in the back row."

He looked up and picking on a young girl sitting remote in the back row began his lecture. The noise continued, but was definitely declining. As it grew quieter, a girl sitting near the front shouted out.

"Give us a shag!"

He remembered her from last year. She was slightly coarse in appearance, but had a full figure that was difficult to ignore. At that time, her request had virtually destroyed the lecture and it had taken him several minutes to become coherent again, much to the amusement of his audience.

This time though he barely gave her a glance, but stoically kept addressing the distant girl in the back row. The renewed hubbub declined again.

It went well. He realised that it was because he felt so much better within himself, combined with a piece of luck that the topic was one he was so familiar with. There were a few paper darts and a few more disruptive attempts to put him off his stride, but he soldiered manfully through it and even felt that the lecture had been quite educational.

His greatest reward was when a few of the more eager students came up after the lecture to ask questions and for clarification. This had never happened last year, when even the most enthusiastic students had considered him to be little more than a joke.

He returned to his room to continue the work with Douglas feeling quite elated. When he walked into his room, he noticed that the white board had the same scribblings, as when he left, and that the A4 pad, in front of Grant was still blank. Douglas' face wore a gaunt distracted look. The death of his foster-brother was clearly on his mind again. Kevin stifled an urge to ask what was wrong and instead sought in his mind, desperately, for something neutral to say.

"Non-standard analysis!"

"I beg your pardon," said Douglas, coming out of his dark reverie.

"It is something that occurred to me during the lecture," lied Kevin, "We could use non-standard analysis in predicting where this is leading us. We could even use it in some of the proofs. It would be controversial, but would make progress a lot faster."

Douglas Grant stared at Kevin. Non-standard analysis was an attempt in the 1960's to reintroduce infinitesimals, the infinitely small, back into mathematics. Infinitesimals had been used by Isaac Newton and other 18th century mathematicians in their conceptually simple, brilliant, incredibly useful, but very flaky, basis for calculus. Infinitesimals had been cast into the outer darkness by 19th century mathematicians as fundamentally unsound and leading to contradictions. They had replaced it with a rigorous, but convoluted, opaque and didactically nearly useless alternative. Kevin was right. If they used infinitesimals they could move forward much faster. There was a greater chance of error and it would certainly be controversial, but Bill Draper thrived on controversy. He would love it.

"You could be right," replied Douglas after some hesitation, his face beginning to light up, "In fact, I think that it is a very good idea."

Kevin was relieved to see that Douglas was again focussing on the mathematics and was rather pleased with himself that Douglas was latching on to the idea so strongly. It was a method that left a terrible mess behind it, but Kevin could then spend many happy years putting it on to a sounder footing. As a mathematician, who liked rigorous proofs, he was far from convinced about non-standard analysis, but its utility was indisputable. He had thought about it briefly during the week, but had brought it up now mainly to give Douglas something immediate to think about.

In the hour before lunch, they set to work again exploring the possibilities of this new avenue. By the time they went for sandwiches, they had already seen that further significant progress could be made.

CHAPTER 9

Ella was sitting down enjoying an afternoon cup of tea. She had just come back from work and was now relaxing. She loved the comfort of Kevin's little house.

Although Kevin had a TV and video player, she had yet to see him use them. This pleased her because she did not like TV herself and also she was very afraid that her case could come up. He did not regularly read any newspapers, though Ella herself was looking at some at work to check if she had a mention. There were mentions, but it was now small paragraphs in the inside pages and usually about the implications for the police, who were criticised for their lack of vigour in the initial stages of the investigation with the often stated implication that it was because the victim had been black. Ella did not enjoy reading them. Sometimes there would be a picture of the victim, showing him full of life and with what should have been a future ahead of him. Once there were separate pictures of Johnny and her. The one of her was enlarged from a school class photograph taken about five years ago and was thankfully blurred and unrecognisable.

There suddenly came a sharp knock at the door. Ella's senses were immediately alert. Standing in the far corner of the room, she could just see the back of the visitor through the side of the bay window. She thought she recognised him and felt surprised that he should be calling at this time.

She went into the hall and cautiously opened the door. She had been right. Standing there was Richard Murdoch, but instead of being his normal dapper self, he looked dishevelled and his eyes had a wild look to them and were red-rimmed. His face was distorted in rage.

"Hullo, bitch!" he snapped, "I suppose you think that your very clever stitching up Kevin."

Ella stared at him, his dishevelled state, his abusive language, his wild accusation. She had an urge just to slam the door in his face. Instead, she stood there coolly appraising him, her cold blue eyes flashing.

"I think that you had better explain yourself." she said, "Why don't you come in?"

"Afraid the neighbours would hear?" he sneered.

"Go ahead," she replied, "Shout it at the top of your voice, but if it's not true, then I will sue you for slander."

He hesitated then, half-tempted to call her bluff, but not really wanting to make a scene.

"Alright," he said storming into the hall and following her into the front sitting room, "But, I know what you are up to, if you cohabit with Kevin for six months then you can lay claim to half his property."

"Firstly, I do not think that you are right and, secondly, I pay rent," she answered, "Such a rule certainly wouldn't apply to tenants."

Rich looked a bit confused by this. He had obviously not expected her to be paying anything. There was the hint of a sheepish look coming into his eyes.

Ella was searching her mind as to why he was in such a state and suddenly a terrible thought came into her mind.

"Nothing has happened to Kevin has it?"

"No! Of course not." he answered. He was starting to look more normal and was clearly increasingly embarrassed by his position.

"Look, I'm sorry, but I am out of order. I must go."

"No, you don't!" she retorted, "First, I insist that you have a cup of tea, while I explain why a woman like me is in love with a man like Kevin. And then you can explain why you have come round here making such wild accusations."

Richard's mood had changed totally. The anger had gone. Now he just looked very upset and abashed. Ella passed him the mug of tea and then sat opposite him, her deep blue eyes locking on to him. The silence stretched out as Ella let him squirm.

"A short time ago," she began at last, "I would have considered someone like Kevin as no more than a joke. I was interested in strong hard men who would lift me out of the poverty of that estate. I succeeded. I suppose I became a gangster's moll. There was, of course, the violence and exploitation against me, but I had expected that. What surprised me was how much I should care about others. How I hated the casual brutality and disdain towards those around us. Worst of all, was my contribution. This man was bad, but with me egging him on he was worse. Part of me saw us as a romantic Bonnie and Clyde couple; another part rejected totally the hurt to others that we were causing."

She paused and took a sip of her tea. Richard sat quietly. The embarrassment had gone, but his face showed some deep hurt that the previous anger had masked. Ella considered carefully how she would continue. She did not want to say too much that might reveal who she was, but she wanted Richard on her side.

"Then we hurt someone rather badly. I probably realised at that point that I could not live with this life. Even then I might have continued, with the romance and the reality coming into sharper and sharper conflict. I would have probably ended up a total druggy."

She stopped again to take another sip of tea.

"How badly was this other person hurt?" asked Richard.

"Quite badly." she responded without further elaboration.

"Something else then happened. I suddenly found myself with a lot of time to think."

"Prison?" queried Richard.

"Prison, sickness, it was neither of those, but similar." she answered enigmatically. In her mind's eye, the blackness surrounded and engulfed her. There came an orange flickering light and she was face to face with the black eyes of death. A maggot was crawling from one of the nostrils.

"I met Kevin by accident. He is not dangerous or bad, but is incredibly comforting. He is what I need."

"I am sorry," said Richard, "I had no right to demand an answer."

He hesitated for a moment and then continued.

"You are right, something has upset me and it has nothing to do with you or Kevin. I suppose I just had to strike out and you were convenient. To make things worse, I am afraid that I can't tell you what it is, which does not seem fair now. Please accept my apologies for my behaviour."

Ella smiled. She now knew that Murdoch's odd behaviour was nothing to do with her. The rest she didn't need to know, except to satisfy a gnawing curiosity.

"Don't worry," she said, "I won't pretend that I am not curious, but it is your business and I accept your apology. "

"Is it OK to ask about your family?" she continued.

The relief on Richard's face answered her question. He proceeded to tell her about his two daughters, aged 8 and 10, who were attending a private school in Bristol.

"They're beautiful girls." he effused. "And they're so happy and lively."

"Does your wife work?" asked Ella.

A slight cloud passed over Richard's face.

"She was working until about six months ago as the manager of an estate agent. Unfortunately, she lost her job when her boss suddenly died. It was rather a tricky time, because shortly afterwards Draper began to put the pressure on me and was making it quite clear that he wanted me out. Fortunately, I am in the union and they sorted him out. Though he began having a go at poor Kevin after that."

"I was sorry about Kevin, but with kids in a private school and with a big mortgage, you could imagine what a disaster it would have been if we had both lost our jobs. At present, Margaret, that's my wife, says that we are just about managing; especially, as she has been able to pick up some consultancy work."

They then chatted together about more general things and Richard gave some background information about himself. His parents had not been particularly well off and his father had worked as a railwayman. However, he had won a scholarship to a private school. He had gone to Durham University where he had met his wife.

"She is still a very beautiful woman." he said, "But then she was a total stunner. All of the young men were making a play for her, but I was the one she chose." he said proudly.

"The problem with raising a family and trying to make ends meet is that one can lose some of that intimate contact with one's partner and that there is so little opportunity to simply have fun together. It is so easy to drift apart." he added, regretfully.

He fell silent and the pain and anguish in his face grew. Ella allowed the silence to stretch out and then filled it by offering him more tea. She then spoke about her own background and her dislike for her mother.

It was well after four o'clock when Richard finally left. She saw him to the front door and watched him go. He crossed the street and turned up the side street diagonally opposite. As Ella turned back to the door she caught a movement of the curtain in the house next to Kevin's.

"There goes my reputation," she thought ruefully, "Men visitors in the afternoon!"

Kevin arrived back just before six o'clock. He was in high spirits, as he had had another good day. He explained to Ella how well his lecture had gone. Ella then told him of Richard's mysterious visit and that he looked more upset than ill.

"Have you met his wife?" asked Ella.

"Yes." replied Kevin, reddening.

"So, she is that good looking." smiled Ella and Kevin reddened further.

"Oh, Kevin," she laughed, "I do love you. You're so straightforward."

"Anyway," she added, "From what Richard said I am sure that she would have a similar effect on other men."

CHAPTER 10

Karen Reading sat back on the floor. She was in her father's office in the big house they had shared near the Downs. Douglas couldn't see her tonight, so she was taking the opportunity to sort out more of her father's things. Her father's stern faced lawyer had guided her on putting the business in order, but she herself had ignored the office, at first because she was too upset and then, just as her strength was returning, because of Douglas' tragedy.

The office was a converted bedroom and was quite large being roughly 12 by 24 feet. A substantial well-polished mahogany desk sat at the far end from the door and behind it was a matching office chair and sober, velvet curtains drawn over a window that stretched almost the full length of the wall. On one long wall were three filing cabinets and on the other built-in bookshelves. She hauled open the bottom drawer of one of the filing cabinets. In it were some old technical brochures and a large shoebox. Curious, she opened the box up. In it were about a dozen videos. Most had a commercial packaging and from their covers contained pornographic material.

Karen sat back. She knew the stories about her father, but they gelled so little with the man that she knew that she could just ignore them. Now though she was coming face to face with that part of him that he had kept hidden from her. There were two videos in the box that were clearly home recorded and simply had dates on them. She picked one up handling it, gingerly, as if it might blow up. They were probably just copies of commercial videos she thought to herself, without conviction. She knew what might be on them and how it could forever mar her image of her father, but she had to know.

In trepidation, she went downstairs and placed the tape into the video player in the sitting room. She turned the television on and waited.

It lasted an hour, but Karen's face was streaming with tears after the first five minutes. It had featured two girls and a man. The man was her father and the girls looked barely sixteen. It was not just what they did, but how her father behaved. The girls were clearly not experienced. The tape had begun with them dressed in lingerie, which had clearly been the initial deal. Then fully recorded on tape was how he gradually got them to do more and more by a mixture of bullying and money.

Karen felt very sick. It was worse than she had expected. Sex, even perverted sex would have been more tolerable, but it was the fact that he had actually taped the corruption process, that he had derived pleasure from actually watching young girls being destroyed. She thought of how their lives would now be blighted forever and how that very fact had given him pleasure. Gaining knowledge was a one-way street. It was impossible to unknow something and she now knew that her father had been a monster.

She got up from the leather easy chair and looked around the large comfortable room that had been their sitting room. She thought of his laughter and his gentleness to her, while all the time he had been subverting and destroying other girls just like her. She walked into the hall and looked into the mirror that hung there. Her own face looked back and within her's was his. It had often been said that she looked like her father.

"Oh, Daddy!" she thought, tears still streaming down her face, "What else of you is in me?"

Richard Murdoch got up from the armchair.

"Thanks very much for the tea and the chat," he said to Ella, "It has really cheered me up."

Ella saw him to the door. It was Thursday afternoon and Richard had astonished her by turning up again. This time he had been civil from the beginning and still very contrite about his behaviour on Monday. He had stayed for about three-quarters of an hour. Ella enjoyed his company. He was very down to earth compared to Kevin. Although he had not actually made a pass at her, Ella still picked up an interest from him that seemed sexual. Considering the renowned beauty of his wife, Ella found this both flattering and surprising.

She followed him down the incredibly short garden path. It was just over a yard long and the tiny garden had been concreted over, though some others in the street still bravely tried to cultivate flowers. After saying her farewell, she turned and found herself face to face with the next door neighbour.

She was a small woman, even smaller than Ella, and of light build. She was in her early sixties and had long, grey hair that just failed to meet the shoulders. Her face was quite angular, but the old skin, although lined still appeared soft. Her eyes were a pale, nearly watery blue. There was a nervousness and jerkiness about her that conveyed fear.

"Good afternoon," said the woman, politely, "I have seen you here for about two weeks now and I thought it was time that I introduced myself. I'm Rosemary Brown."

"And I'm Ella Slater", responded Ella, entering into the spirit of the exchange. "Perhaps you would like to join me for a cup of tea."

Rosemary Brown looked surprised, but readily agreed.

They went into Kevin's small sitting room, where two cups and a bowl of sugar still sat on a low table in front of the two easy chairs. Ella was not quite sure why she had invited this woman in. Certainly, one reason was to demonstrate that she was not a person to fear and another was to show, as far as possible, that she and Richard had been together in the sitting room having tea and not upstairs having each other.

"I have just had some tea with my friend." said Ella, "But fortunately I am a tea addict."

At first, the conversation was strained and mainly concerned the weather. It livened up a bit when Ella asked Rosemary if she had any family. Rosemary had been married, but her husband had died several years ago, when still quite young. She had one married daughter who lived in London and now had her own family.

All the time that she was talking Ella would catch the woman glancing nervously out of the window.

"Are you looking for someone?" Ella finally asked.

Rosemary started guiltily. She started to mutter, disjointedly, about a friend possibly coming and then she seemed to come to a decision.

"I'm sorry," she said, "You'll probably just think that I am a lonely, silly old woman, but, to be honest, I am afraid. I think that someone is watching me and intends me harm. You see I am a Jew."

Ella looked at her blankly.

"There are many Jews in Bristol," she said, "Why should they pick on you?"

"I know. It sounds very silly, especially, when I try and explain it. I don't have a Jewish name, I don't join pro-Israeli protests and I don't even attend synagogue. But I am a friend of Rachel Silverman."

Ella looked at her, her face a study in puzzlement.

"Sorry, so what?" she finally managed.

"Oh, I am sorry, you wouldn't know her, but she was the woman who was attacked and badly beaten up Sunday night."

The images and feelings of that night came back to Ella. Her total despair when she thought that it was all over, the sour taste of defeat. She made a mental note to herself not to get so emotionally laid back.

"It was terrible!" Rosemary continued, "The attackers had written on her living room wall, in big black letters - DIE JEWISH BITCH- Her injuries are awful. Her face is nearly unrecognisable and she has suffered some nasty internal injuries. She will need to stay in hospital for another three weeks, at least. And you know how they try and rush people out these days."

Ella stared thoughtfully at Rosemary. It did sound extremely unpleasant and it had almost certainly unnerved Rosemary. A lonely widow living on her own, no wonder she was subject to fearful fancies.

"I know you think that I am being foolish. After all, most people don't even know that I am Jewish. But I have seen him watching my house. More than once."

"There are many reasons why someone could stand in the street," replied Ella, trying to not sound patronising.

"But one day a week before the attack, we had a coffee morning at Rachel's, I saw him then. I thought that he was furtive and trying to avoid being seen by us. He wrapped his grey scarf up around his face to hide it. That is why I remember him."

It was like an electric shock going through Ella. Now she was taking this woman very seriously indeed. She remembered that muffled figure that she saw her first full day here.

"Hmm," she said, "I think I once saw someone fitting your description and he appeared to be watching your house. Or Kevin's" she added. "After all, though I am paler than most people you could meet to a fascist I'm still a black. But it was before the attack on your friend."

Rosemary stared her face had gone grey and she looked visibly upset. She had wanted to be told that she was just a foolish old woman, but she now sensed that Ella believed her.

"It is probably just me living on my own. One can magnify the tiniest thing." she finally murmured weakly, in a last desperate effort to have Ella dismiss her fears.

"Maybe," replied Ella, "But I think that we should treat this as potentially serious. In my view, there is a very real risk."

"What I suggest is that we both look out for this loiterer or, indeed, anyone else who is behaving suspiciously and perhaps even keep a record of it. If we think that it looks threatening then such a record would help us convince the police that there is a real problem." Not that Ella would dream of going to the police, but she felt that Rosemary would see this as perfectly normal.

"Yes, I suppose that you are right," said Rosemary, still looking very worried.

"I suggest also," said Ella, "that you make sure that your house is always secure and that you check any visitors before opening the door."

"When did you last see this man?" asked Ella, as an afterthought.

Rosemary gulped. "Just before stepping outside to meet you. He was there for at least five minutes, but he disappeared when you opened your door to let your visitor out."

"Then I think that I am right this has to be taken most seriously." responded Ella.

As Rosemary left, Ella felt guilty about winding her up, but, to be honest, she felt concerned herself. There were more things to worry about than just deranged fascists. It would be useful to have someone watching for any unusual activity around Kevin's house.

CHAPTER 11

Sarah Morgan took a sip of her gin and tonic. She was a quiet, reserved woman, who did not like to drink too much. Sitting next to her was her sister-in-law Emily Harris, who was neither quiet nor reserved. Emily thoroughly enjoyed her drink and had already downed three rum and cokes. She was in an animated discussion with the young woman opposite. Emily was telling her about her holidays in her caravan.

Emily's conversation partner both fascinated and disconcerted Sarah. She had African features, but an incredibly pale skin scattered with freckles. Above her left eye was a prominent brown birthmark and her face also carried several nearly healed cuts and scratches. Her hair was very fair, but tightly curled and sprayed about her head chaotically. It was the eyes that were the most disturbing. They were an intense blue, nearly unblinking and seemed to strip your mind bare, exposing all your inner thoughts. They made Sarah shiver slightly.

The man with this troubling woman was jarringly different. His eyes would carefully avoid all others. He clung on to his half-drunk glass of beer, as if it were a life belt. He was somewhat older than his companion and had a slightly fat, soft look. His hair was cut quite short, brown with gentle curls. He wore a distinctly shabby old suit that did not quite fit.

Sarah noticed that when it came to their round, it was the woman, who got up to challenge the crowded bar. Sarah would have preferred the relative quiet of the lounge of the Good Companions pub, but Emily loved the noise and bustle of the public bar. She suspected that Emily even relished the lewd comments and the amorous attentions of the young men. Sitting on her other side was her nephew Paul Harris. His arm was around a fine featured and pretty, but very delicate and young looking girl. Paul worked at Ashbury's and he had invited the disturbing woman because they worked together.

Sitting next to the quiet man was her brother, Gavin, Emily's husband. He was not a talkative person himself and, since, he had been made redundant by Rolls Royce his self-confidence had collapsed. The two sat together in silence.

Paul looked up from his quiet mutterings to the young girl with him to speak to his father, trying to draw him out.

"How are the horses doing pop?" he asked, cheerfully, "Still losing money?"

His father grunted noncommittally.

"Do you do the horses?" said the quiet man beside him. "I never bet on them, but I used to love watching them and working out how to bet to make the most money in the afternoon. I know nothing of form. I used to go just by the odds. I think I have a system that could, usually, win."

Paul's father laughed.

"You wouldn't be the first to have a system, but you would be the first if it worked. The whole thing is rigged so that the bookies win. Mind you, it can go very badly wrong for them. If you were to walk in to a bookie's shop and bet a pile on an outsider, then the bookie should lay the bet off. That means he should bet on the same horse with Ladbrokes or another national bookmaker so that if the horse does win he can cover the bet. One year an outsider called Ben Nevis won the Grand National. Two small betting shops near the foot of Ben Nevis had not laid those bets off and were ruined. All the locals had bet on it for the name"

"That's what I do now. I work part-time in the bookies, just up the road here and my job is to spot when we're exposed and lay the bets off." He looked sadly at his hands. "Used to be a toolmaker at Rolls Royce - that was a real job. But Thatcher and her crew saw us off. Ten years ago now it was."

"Still it must be a responsible job," said Kevin, "Get it wrong and your boss would be ruined."

"Certainly is," replied Paul's father, "Now the man, who did the job before me..."

Sarah let the conversation fade into the general cacophony of a pub full of people. She was looking round the table. Most glasses were well down and it was her round. She eyed the bar with consternation. It was crowded with a group of noisy, young men. She took orders and got up to go to the bar.

"I'll give you a hand," volunteered the disconcerting woman, rising from her chair. Sarah felt very grateful.

Ella led the way to the bar and seemingly effortlessly moved to the front. One of the young men spoke to her and Ella said something back and the young man laughed loudly. Removing the young man's hand from her backside, she placed the order. Sarah was just able to get near enough to pass her the money.

The drinks safely on the table, Sarah sank back thankfully into her seat. The strange woman, Ella, had handled with casual ease, even a certain enjoyment, what she would have found a difficult situation.

Afterwards, Emily invited everyone back to her small house. They passed through a tiny entrance hall with stairs leading off it to the upper floor and then into a small living room into which they all crowded. Another tiny hall led to the backdoor and a small kitchen. The living room was comfortably, though rather densely furnished, and exuded a warm cosiness.

Ella was enjoying herself. The only discordant note was that Emily was one of those people, who always had the TV on, but proceeded to ignore it as they engaged in vigorous conversations. For everyone else, there was the difficult task of trying to do two things at once and not succeeding very well with either. She noticed that Kevin was still engaged in an earnest conversation with Emily's husband. He was noticeably more talkative than usual.

Emily turned to talk to her sister-in-law and Ella's eyes wandered back to the TV. She came face to face with the young man she had helped kill. She involuntarily drew in breath, but in all the general hubbub, no one seemed to notice. It was clearly a documentary on the murder, because the next picture was one of Johnny and that was followed by her blurred old school photograph.

"What a totally hopeless picture." said Paul, "I could be sitting right next to her and never recognise her from that."

"The police have really cocked it up," he continued, "They don't give a toss, because the victim's black."

"That's not fair!" exclaimed Fiona, the elfin-faced girl beside him, "There were four, drug related gang killings in Manchester in that month. It was only natural that they should think that this was another one."

"You're only saying that because your dad's one of them," said Paul, "But they got really caught out on this one. That bloke was one of the few heroes that the Church of England still had. He was known by all the local bigwigs."

Fortunately, the sound was turned down and the program moved on to a different topic. All around Ella everything carried on as before: Kevin was still in a deep conversation with Gavin, Sarah was nodding in an interested way as Emily chattered away, Paul having perhaps realised that he had antagonised Fiona was whispering into her ear and making her giggle. For Ella it had been like a moment of silence, time out or perhaps better words were time in; a time to remember what she had done. From deep within her it arose again the iron willpower that had seen her through. She had had a month of doomed darkness to remember. She was moving on.

"You said earlier that you had some photographs of your caravan?" she asked Emily. Emily looked delighted and fetched two photo albums from the bookshelf. For Ella the bad moment was washed away as Emily cheerfully told the story related to each picture; pictures of her, Gavin, Sarah, Paul and others Ella did not know, standing by the caravan, on sunny beaches with a blue sea behind, laughing, happy, full of life.

By the time Kevin and Ella started their walk home, it was after one o'clock in the morning. The night was clear with a strong hint of a winter chill. On Horfield estate, the streetlights were dim and far apart. They passed a whole block that had been demolished.

"Concrete cancer." explained Kevin, "They had to knock them all down because they weren't safe anymore. There are some nice new houses towards the top of the estate."

Ella glanced nervously at a group of about five youths, who were walking down the road towards them. On one side was a row of totally dark houses and on the other the empty expanse of the demolished block. The youths drew level and she noticed that one was carrying what looked like an iron bar.

Kevin was totally oblivious, anaesthetised by drink. He was looking out over the vanished block. "Look!" he said, "There's the plough." he pointed to an arc of bright stars, "I find it so much easier to identify the constellations, when you're in a city because only the bright stars are visible. Out in the countryside, there are so many stars I can't tell one from another."

"Stay out of the light." one youth cautioned another as they went past. The youths continued up the road intent on their mission and ignoring the couple standing hand in hand staring at the sky.

"Somewhere up there," said Kevin, "There are probably intelligent beings looking at their sky and wondering."

"Well, I hope that they're more sober than you," laughed Ella, "Come on, let's go home."

Paul Harris listened to the deep breathing of the girl lying beside him. Her soft small body lay in his arms. She had though been a passionate lover, slightly more experienced than he expected - but that was modern women. It was a lucky thing for him that her parents didn't know how liberal his parents were. Her father was very strict.

Thinking of her father, reminded him that he had almost blown it criticising the police. Just in time, he noticed that she was becoming upset.

"Mind you," he thought to himself, "They had made a real mess of it. And that picture of the girl they were after, surely they could find a better one. What could you tell from it? She had a boff, nothing else."

Somewhere in his head he heard a TV announcer saying that she had Afro-Caribbean features, but was very pale. He had must have heard a report sometime when his mum had been drawing a breath. Strange, the new girl Ella had Afro-Caribbean features and was very pale. She also had a distinctive boff and spoke with a strong Manchester accent.

"What an interesting fantasy." he thought, as he drifted off into deep sleep.

CHAPTER 12

Sunday morning dawned painfully for Kevin. He was not used to alcohol, and his modest excess of the night before had left him with a headache and a dry mouth.

Ella walked in. She was already dressed and was looking unreasonably bright and cheerful.

"Come on, Kevin!" she said, much too loudly, "Time for breakfast, the table is all set and then I will take you for a morning walk."

Kevin groaned. He looked at the time. It was only eight o'clock.

After breakfast, Ella was as good as her word about the walk.

A finger of countryside still penetrated into Bristol and stretched all the way to Mueller Road, less than a mile from where Kevin lived. Emily had told Ella about it the previous evening and she was very keen to explore it. Kevin had had no idea that it existed and was surprised when Ella led him down Ashley Down Road cut through to Mueller Road, down under a railway bridge and up a grassy embankment on the other side.

After a stiff climb that left Kevin sweating and panting for breath, they found themselves on a single-track road that led to a concrete tower, bristling with radio communications equipment. Kevin wondered vaguely about articles he had read on the dangers of electromagnetic radiation. The road abruptly ended at the radio tower and they found themselves on a path that passed the concrete remnants of a series of Second World War dugouts and bunkers. Ella said that Emily had told her that it had been the site of an anti-aircraft gun known locally as Purdown Percy.

Just beyond these structures they found out why this was a prime site for such a defensive structure. They were on the crest of a hill and stretched out below them was the whole of Bristol. Any aircraft attacking the city would have exposed itself to fire from this position.

Kevin felt a lot better. The morning coffee and then the fresh air, with its slightly chill wind of an overcast, but dry morning, had revived him. He took in the sight and turned to Ella and kissed her. Kevin had never felt so relaxed with any woman. Even his ever-present insecurity convinced that it could not last, would not detract from the happiness of this moment.

Far below them, hidden at the bottom of the hill, arose the hum of the M32 motorway, which appeared from under the hill before merging into the city beyond. Even at this time on a Sunday morning, the cars were becoming more frequent. They turned to descend the hill and Kevin saw in the distance a spectacular orange edifice set on a rocky prominence, looking like one of mad Ludwig's Bavarian castles.

"Emily said that is Stoke Hospital, which used to be a mental home, but has now been converted to luxury flats." stated Ella, "Oh, and we have got to watch out for the headless horseman, he is meant to haunt this parkland."

Kevin noted somewhat guiltily that Ella seemed to have learned more about their environs in the three weeks that she had been here than he had in his four years.

Below them toiling up the hill towards them was a hooded man, continuously circled by a black and white collie dog. As he got nearer he lowered the hood, revealing short grey hair. He greeted them, revealing a distinct Scottish accent.

"We're new here," said Ella, stopping, "A friend said that this was a good area for a nice circular walk."

"It certainly is." answered the man.

"If you go down to the bottom of the valley, past Duchess pond," he said pointing to an expanse of water lying at the bottom of the valley to the right of the path. "Then keep going towards that big building on the hill. Just before you get there turn to your left and there's a path that takes you through the wood, up a series of steps and then turns left again at the top. You can then carry straight on along that path, back here or you can turn right into the woods. If you keep to the right edge in the woods, you eventually come to a main path, which runs through the woods. Turn left on to that path and that will also bring you back here."

Thanking the man they walked on down the hill and up the other side. By the time they came to the branch, where they could choose to go into the woods, Kevin was sweating profusely. The walk up the other side of the valley had taken its toll on him. However, Ella's enthusiasm for taking the longer walk through the woods was not to be curtailed and Kevin found himself reluctantly agreeing.

The woods were gloomy, but not unpleasant. There were some trees that had clearly been blown over several years before, with massive up-ended roots. One of these trees had bravely put up vertical branches from its horizontal trunk with the dying summer leaves still clinging to them. They stood and looked at it and Kevin felt Ella shiver. Tears were coming into her eyes.

"That's like me," she declared, "Still trying, though it doesn't realise that it's doomed."

Kevin held her tighter and her tear filled eyes looked into his. She kissed him passionately and clung to him.

"Kevin," she said, staring straight into his eyes, "You are the best thing that has ever happened to me."

Kevin felt both warmed and baffled by this. His self-image could not see himself as being that important to anyone.

For the rest of the walk Ella held Kevin's arm and pulled herself close to him. Kevin was conscious of her body even through their thick warm clothes. By the time that they got back to Kevin's house they had been away for nearly three hours. However, despite it being nearly lunchtime, Ella led Kevin straight upstairs to bed. It was another hour before they finally descended to eat.

CHAPTER 13

It was late on Monday afternoon and Kevin would be home soon. Ella sat pondering over Richard Murdoch's latest visit. She had got home from Ashbury's just after three thirty and Richard had knocked on the door before the kettle boiled. He had stayed for about an hour and had been friendly, courteous and even witty, but he left Ella with a strong, but odd, feeling that he was coming for comfort. Underneath his ever-present bonhomie there seemed to be strong emotions churning.

Her mind then turned to herself and Kevin. Her feelings for him had not diminished. If anything they had got even stronger. She thought then of her previous boyfriend. He had literally led her into hell. The two were so different and yet she feared that there was one common thread - her own childish romanticism. In her imagination she turned both of them into men that they were not. Johnny was the romantic gangster hero and Kevin was the quiet, but intensely loyal lover. Johnny had been no hero and she knew that Kevin's loyalty would not survive knowing the truth about her. Better to live for the present and enjoy it while she could, a darker day could be close.

Her musings were interrupted by the arrival of Kevin. He looked tired and grey. He gave her a distinctly cursory kiss and sat down. There was a gloom about him that she had not seen since their first Monday together when he had gone back to the University.

"Kevin," she said, taking his black mood head-on, "What's the matter?"

"It's Draper!" he exclaimed, "He is due back on Wednesday, "All the old feelings are coming back. I am dreading having to face that man again."

"Oh Kevin, you're in a much stronger position than you were three weeks ago." declared Ella, with some exasperation.

"This Grant is not planning to ditch you, is he?" she added, as a sudden doubt crossed her mind.

"Oh no!" exclaimed Kevin, "He's very supportive."

"Then there is no problem," said Ella with finality, "I will go and get a couple of fresh pizzas from the Pizzeria on Gloucester Road and in the meantime you can open a bottle of red wine and set the table."

Ella's strategy worked. The mixture of alcohol and her reminders to him about how well the work had been going did manage to restore him to a better humour. After the meal, they curled up together on the couch and listened to one of Kevin's favourites, a Simon and Garfunkel album. Ella enjoyed the gentle music and the closeness of Kevin.

Some weekdays are better than others at work, for Ella this had not been one of the better days. Time had dragged. There had been enough stacking and refilling of shelves to be irritating, but not enough to make the time pass quickly. Unusually, her supervisor had been tetchy and irritable, which made each request more of an imposition than it really was.

The steady drizzle had soaked her, despite the shortness of the walk from the bus stop to Kevin's front gate. Wet clothes off, a cup of tea and mental distance from the morning that was what she needed. She took the one and a half steps up the tiny garden path to the front door. Her cold hands fumbled with the key. At last it was in the lock.

"Excuse me, miss!"

Ella turned. Standing there at the gate, only a yard from her, the rain dripping of his regulation rainwear, was a young policeman.

He was over a foot taller than Ella and all the official clothing could not disguise the muscle that lay underneath.

Again caught by surprise and off-guard, Ella's trivial troubles vanished to be replaced by an overwhelming feeling of despair and defeat.

"Sorry to alarm you miss," continued the young policeman, "But we have had a report of an intruder in your house."

Ella caught sight of Rosemary's face looking out of the bay window next door. Well she had only herself to blame. She had deliberately got the lonely woman worked up.

"If you don't mind, I think that I had better come in with you."

"Yes, of course," said Ella, desperately trying to sound reassured, "Thank you very much."

She turned back to the door, twisted the key in the lock and opened the door.

She gasped. Heading out through the kitchen she caught a glimpse of a heavy male figure clad in black trousers, a black top and a black, woollen hat.

"Hey you! Stop! Police"

The policeman bounded past after the retreating figure.

Ella stood dumbfounded. She turned into the living room and came face to face with a new shock. On the wall above the fireplace was written in large black letters:

"DIE NIGGER BITCH"

The fact that the threat was aimed at her personally shook even Ella.

The policeman returned apologising that the intruder had escaped, but that he was radioing for support. However, when he saw the message above the fireplace he stopped dead. He was back on the radio.

Ella was feeling tired. The last two hours had been chaotic. Further police had arrived, including three scene of crime personnel in their disposable white overalls. The interview with the two CID officers was carried out in the tiny backroom. Fortunately for Ella they were far more interested in what she had been doing since coming to Bristol than before.

When they asked for her previous address, she had to speak of a hostel, but that she had been too confused at the time due to a mental breakdown to remember where it was. She said that her life had been very disorganised until she had met Kevin. They accepted her vague generalisations with obvious scepticism, but were much more penetrating about her relationships since coming to Bristol.

They apologetically asked if she had had any other lovers and what work she had been doing.

Ella could tell them the truth of her activities since coming to Bristol and noted how surprisingly refreshing it was.

The interview was about half way through when Kevin appeared at the doorway. He looked pale and shaken. He was dwarfed by the police constable standing behind him.

"Ella what happened? Are you OK?"

Ella stood up and ignoring the two CID men went to him.

"It's OK dear," she said gently, "Thanks to Rosemary next door and the prompt action of the police, I am unhurt. Otherwise, though, I could have ended up like that poor Jewish woman.

The two CID men looked up in surprise.

"You know about her?" queried the senior officer. He was an overweight man in his late thirties with a strongly receding hairline and a balding patch at the front of his head.

"Oh yes," replied Ella, "Rosemary next door told me. She was afraid that she was being watched. I, myself, have on two occasions seen a suspicious looking man apparently watching our houses."

"Could you describe him?" asked the plump officer.

"I can," responded Ella, "But he was too small and weedy to be the man I saw in the house."

The CID men were very interested then as she described the figure and when she had seen him.

They were the last police to leave the house and when they did they went straight next door to talk to Rosemary.

Ella heard them knock and the door opening, short mumble of voices and then silence. She felt worried. The last thing she had wanted was to have the attention of the police. If they began making any enquiries about her background, they would soon find out that she was not Ella Slater. She had a terrible feeling that the clock had started ticking.

"What bad luck!" she thought, "And it was bad luck. Why should a demented fascist pick on her when there were at least three distinctly black, black families in the street?"

She found Kevin in the front room staring aghast at the slogan above the fireplace.

"Don't worry," said Ella, firmly, "I will paint it out tomorrow."

She found herself looking at Kevin, his anxious expression, his short dark curls, his gentleness, his vulnerability and the love he was giving her. The tears came suddenly flooding down her face and she held him to her. It would all soon end. She could survive it. She had before, but the loss.

Finally, she let him go.

"Kevin, could you make the tea. I need to sit for a bit. It has shaken me."

She sat down on the couch in the front room trying to ignore the slogan above the fireplace. Within five minutes she had gone to hunt for a pot of white gloss to blot it out.

Ella invited Rosemary for tea. She had felt it was the least that she could do to show her gratitude.

"I knew that you weren't back," Rosemary said, bravely eating Kevin's soggy omelette and soggier chips, "But I saw this man in your back garden and then I heard a sound that could have been breaking glass and the back door opening and shutting. I almost didn't call the police, I am so afraid of being viewed as a foolish old woman. If I had hesitated longer or not rung at all.... It does not bear thinking about."

"Well I'm very glad you did." said Ella, "He was clearly waiting for me to come home and to give me a going over like he did to your poor friend."

"It's very worrying that he is still out there," said Rosemary, "Do you think that the police will get him."

"Oh, I am sure that they will" replied Ella, with more confidence than she actually felt. After all they had not caught her - yet.

CHAPTER 14

Kevin's mouth felt like it was full of sawdust. He had a disorientated floating feeling that was so strong he felt unsteady and liable to fall over at any time.

Douglas Grant was walking beside him. He seemed totally unperturbed.

"I think it would be a good idea to give Bill a rapid overview and then take him into the nuts and bolts. He's a concept man. He'll like that," Douglas Grant spoke slowly and thoughtfully as if he were describing nothing more stressing than boiling an egg.

It was nine o'clock on Thursday morning. Draper had returned yesterday, but by a mixture of good luck and design Kevin had managed to avoid seeing him. Douglas had seen him though and arranged this meeting.

"He was in a foul mood," Douglas had laughed, "I'm afraid our stars are not in the ascendant."

This remark had not helped Kevin's state of mind. They entered the outer office. Sadie sat at her PC, slender and smart. She looked at them coldly.

"The professor is waiting you can go straight in."

"Thank you." said Douglas with a smile, apparently oblivious to Sadie's hostility.

He tapped on the door of the professor's office and walked in with Kevin nearly staggering behind him.

Draper's office was nearly twice the size of everyone else's in the department. As they entered, they were faced with a long table with two chairs on each side. At the head of the table, sitting hard against it was Bill Draper's substantial oak desk and behind him a window and a small table to his right on which sat a desktop PC.

On the wall opposite Draper, was a white board. The two other walls had shelves up to chest height lined with books and journals.

Draper sat at his desk on a comfortable swivel chair.

He was a short thickset man with a square face, a dark moustache and short black hair, with only a hint of grey. He was in his mid-thirties and was clearly healthy and took regular exercise. He had brown questioning eyes and an air of physical and mental presence.

He did not rise when they came in. Nor did he offer them a seat. Douglas Grant took the one on the near side of the desk, closest to Draper. Kevin sank gratefully into the one behind him allowing Douglas to partially obscure him from Draper.

There were no niceties, no offer of coffee, no chit-chat about Draper's holiday or the preceding conference; instead, Draper launched into a scathing and threatening speech.

"I expect people in my department to pull their weight. If they don't, there out! There's no quibble about that."

Draper spoke slowly with a loud clipped voice and only a hint of a northern accent. There was both real anger and menace in his words and Kevin felt himself reeling.

"Murdoch and Sullivan have lost valuable research time covering lectures for you two." continued Draper, "This is not the type of situation I am prepared to tolerate. Nor do I expect personal problems to interfere. This is not a convalescent home. I hope I am making myself clear. I am not afraid to sack those who are inadequate. You Grant have tried my patience to its limit."

His piercing unblinking brown eyes fixed on Kevin, "And you are a bumbling incompetent. This is for you."

A sealed white letter flew across the table and landed neatly in front of Kevin. Kevin looked at it as the blood drained from his face. He felt sick and faint. His hand, seemingly by its own volition, began to move towards it.

"Just a minute!" said Douglas Grant, evenly and calmly, as his hand blocked Kevin's. "You are quite right, Bill, neither of us has pulled his weight recently. There are no excuses for that, we are both paid highly to deliver and we haven't done so. All I ask is a little bit of your time to present before you our latest work. If you think it is a waste of time, then I will save you a lot of time and trouble by resigning. So will Dr Hansen."

Kevin tried to mutter something affirmative, but although his mouth opened and closed, not a sound came out.

"Very well," said Draper, "But I will hold you to that."

"As I said yesterday," began Douglas, evenly, "We are going to describe to you, what we think are the quite significant developments that we have made."

Kevin felt himself going cold and sweaty. He was afraid that he was going to pass out or be sick. Meanwhile, Douglas Grant appeared to have raised imperturbability to an art form. He calmly stood up and walked behind

Kevin and up to the white board.

He picked a dry marker pen out of his pocket and wrote up the words, 'Intermediate complexity conjecture' in strong black letters at the top of the board. The pen was new. He turned to Draper,

"As you know, Bill, this was where I was three weeks ago, when we last discussed it. It was promising, but not promising enough. At that time, as I explained, I felt that I could not continue, so I raised the issue with Dr Hansen -Kevin- to see if he could see a way to develop it further – indeed, to pass the baton on to Kevin."

This brought a disapproving grunt from Draper that Grant ignored.

"However, my discussions with Kevin have so restored my confidence that I intend to carry on - only if you think that I have something to offer of course." The last phrase was added to forestall a further remark from Draper, who had just started to draw breath. "I would also like to emphasise that this was a genuine joint effort, without Dr Hansen's knowledge of this area, it simply would not have gone forward."

"This conjecture is now a theorem." said Douglas pointing to the words he had written. "In addition, we have found three more theorems, which together give us a quantitative handle on self-organisation. Industrially, we are looking at far more intelligent, self -tuneable control circuits. More philosophically, it will give us a handle on both the origin of life and intelligence."

Douglas then moved into a detailed account of how the original conjecture was proved. At first Draper asked hostile questions, which Douglas either ignored or deferred until later. As the proof unfolded though Draper's attitude changed. His questions although penetrating, were expressing a real interest and excitement.

After about forty-five minutes, Draper suddenly raised his hand, "Stop, I want Dr Sullivan in on this, I need his analytical mind to properly assess this."

"Sadie!" he bellowed.

The secretary came cautiously into the room.

"I want Dr Sullivan up here right away." he demanded.

"Dr Sullivan has a lecture in about ten minutes," countered Sadie.

"Then ask him to cancel it. I want him here immediately."

Sadie looked disapproving, but even she was not going to face down Draper. She left the room.

In the hiatus, while waiting for Dr Sullivan, Draper finally offered everyone coffee.

A good sign thought Kevin, who was just beginning to relax a little. Although he was feeling better than at the beginning of the meeting, he still felt unwell and the strain was making him feel very tired. Every so often, he would find his eyes straying to the menacing, white envelope lying in front of him. He marvelled at Grant, who seemed to be showing no signs of strain. Indeed he appeared to be in good humour.

He also felt apprehensive about Dr Sullivan. The man had a very clear mind and if there were holes in the logic of their arguments then Sullivan would find them.

Sullivan entered the room about five minutes after being summoned. He made no comment about his disrupted schedule, but put the cup of coffee that Sadie had given to him on the position opposite Grant and sat down. He then looked up with his sharp blue intelligent eyes at Draper.

He was a man of about fifty, with remnants of very thin, red hair clinging to his head. He had a fair freckly face with a nearly aquiline nose. He was just under six feet tall and looked fairly muscular with no tendency to fat.

Over their coffee, Draper explained what the meeting was about. Draper kept to a fairly neutral attitude. He said that, if true, the discoveries were extremely important, but that it was of the utmost importance that there were no obvious or not so obvious flaws in the arguments.

With no sign of tiredness or irritation, Douglas Grant went back through the details he had already given to Draper and then went on to develop them further.

The rest of the morning went well. Dr Sullivan was, as usual, on form, but his comments and questions strengthened and deepened the initial arguments, they did not erode them.

By the end of the morning, Bill Draper was positively jovial. There was no doubt that he was impressed and pleased with what had been done.

"Right!" exclaimed Draper as he closed the meeting, "Its lunch in the pub, it appears we have something to celebrate."

As he rose, Douglas picked up the envelope in front of Kevin and passed it back to Bill Draper.

"I don't think he will need this now." he said, with the hint of a smile.

Draper looked at the envelope in Grant's hand. For a moment, his face was expressionless and then it broke into a grin.

"Dr Hansen," he said, looking Kevin straight in the eye, "I misjudged you. You have my sincerest apologies."

As he said this, he took the envelope from Douglas, tore it and its contents into several pieces and dropped them into his wastepaper basket.

Kevin felt as if his nerves were screaming, he had to let everybody else stand up first and start to leave the room, before he was able to rise. All morning, the envelope had sat in front of him like an executioner's axe and now it was gone.

CHAPTER 15

Paul Harris stared intently at the tall man in front of him. The man was well built, but overweight and would be formidable in a fight. It was Thursday night and Paul had only come to collect Fiona and take her out for a drink. Instead he found that Fiona's father was intent on giving him the third degree. The man was both suspicious and offensive and Paul was finding it hard to keep his temper. They were standing in the hallway of the Camerons' house a private, semidetached on Filton Avenue, slightly further out of Bristol than Paul's house.

The big man clearly viewed Paul as not the right sort of person for his daughter.

"Yes," agreed Paul, reluctantly, "I did not do well in school, but I am going to start a management trainee course at Ashbury's in March, next year."

The man was really getting to him, but for Fiona's sake he was trying to keep calm. The trouble was he was now giving straight answers to what he felt were blatantly impertinent questions.

"Frankly," continued the father, in his offensive vein, "I would prefer my daughter to go out with someone of more character."

"You mean like a policeman," said Paul, feeling his anger beginning to rise.

"Precisely," said the man, missing the sarcasm, "That takes guts and brains."

"Oh yeah," responded Paul, "Then how come they can't find the Mantree Estate two, while I've already found one of them."

As soon as he said it he regretted it. He had liked the strange woman called Ella. Now, he felt like a traitor.

But Cameron did not let the moment pass. He became interrogative and Paul found himself telling the man his suspicions. Paul desperately tried to play his suspicions down, but in Cameron's eyes' this only lent them credence.

He was, however, still highly sceptical and asked Fiona what she thought when she reappeared from upstairs where she had retreated. She was surprised by the idea, as Paul had not mentioned it to her. He had not intended to mention it to anyone.

"Just a minute," said Cameron, "I have an old newspaper cutting about it here." He began rummaging through an untidy pile of newspapers and cuttings that lay in a pile on a small table by a comfortable looking armchair. Finally with an exclamation of triumph, he picked out a cutting and read out the description of the wanted woman from it.

Fiona looked thoughtful and then she said, excitedly, "It could be her couldn't it Paul. She does have quite a distinctive appearance and she even has a birthmark like the one described in the article. Oh dad, Paul the pair of you could have caught her."

Paul felt sick. The description sounded a perfect match to him. What had he done?

Detective constable Jane Kent stared at the paperwork in front of her.

"Was she getting more than her fair share because she was a woman?" she thought to herself. "After all the police force was still a man's world, even at the start of the new millennium."

It was nine o'clock on a Thursday night and her shift at Southmead police station finished in an hour. Should she stay on to try and get some more of this cleared? Was she ambitious enough? Once she had been.

Her negative thoughts were interrupted by a knock on the open door. She looked up to see the desk sergeant there with PC Cameron hovering behind him.

"Come in," she said, with barely disguised relief.

"I suppose I should be glad that they are not paying me a clerk's wages," she complained, waving at the pile in front of her.

"I know the feeling," sympathised the sergeant, "But Alex, here may be able to liven things up a bit. He has just started his shift and has picked up what could be interesting information"

PC Cameron coughed, self-consciously as the young female DC looked up at him expectantly. She was probably not yet thirty and appeared even younger, with a pale complexion and a pert nose. Her big blue eyes looked him full in the face. He felt envious of her, of the ease with which she seemed to progress up the ranks, though there was no denying her competence.

"I have been given a description of a woman who fits the description of one of those wanted for the Mantree estate killing."

"OK," responded the DC, reaching for the appropriate form to record the details on, "Please sit down, Alex."

"George," she said, addressing the desk sergeant, "Could you dig out the file on this. We must have something."

By the time the desk sergeant returned, Jane had recorded Cameron's information.

She took the thin, brown folder from the sergeant and looked at the two faxed sheets that lay within and scanned them.

."Seems convincing," she said, looking at PC Cameron, "And there is a birthmark in the right place."

"Let's ring Manchester and see what they have to say." She added looking down again at the top sheet in her hand.

She picked out the number from the sheet and tapped it into her phone. Having been transferred to the appropriate person, she began to report on the possible sighting of the suspect, but was clearly interrupted and began listening. At first her face was surprised and then a clear look of disappointment came over it. After about three minutes she put the phone down and looked up at the two men in front of her.

"Sorry, Alex," she said, with genuine regret, "Manchester reports that they have now found two bodies. One is badly decomposed, but is nearly intact and male. It is very likely the missing man, though they are still waiting for dental confirmation. The second body is dispersed and they only have some fragments, but there is definitely another body. They feel that it must be that of the woman."

Alex Cameron visibly sagged and with a mumble left. The desk sergeant turned to follow him.

"George!" shouted Jane stopping him. "Make sure that this goes in the incident book and is brought to the DI's attention tomorrow. The description was so good."

"That was police work," she thought to herself, "You had what seemed a perfect fit with the evidence, but then you found that it was completely wrong."

She turned back to the paperwork in front of her. It had not got any smaller in the last half-hour.

Richard Murdoch was worried. He had met Sadie at ten o'clock in the corridor outside his office on her way for her morning coffee break. He and Sadie got on well together. She saw Richard giving lectures, tutoring and encouraging students and organising his classes. In other words, he was doing his job. Whereas some of the others. They were so precious. They hid in their offices and seemed to be paid for very little.

"It's not fair," she had complained, looking upset, "They do nothing for months and then in one morning they twist the prof around their fingers. Other people do proper work and he... doesn't treat them right."

The last phrase had been mumbled, as if Sadie had suddenly realised that she had said too much. She had then rushed off in some confusion.

Richard thought over the situation. Grant and Kevin had obviously had a good day yesterday. This meant that Draper would probably want to keep them. But Draper would still want to bring down his other man from Manchester. This almost certainly meant that he was back in the firing line again.

He stared out of the window at the autumn scene. The leaves on the trees that had survived the heavy rain had now nearly completely changed colour. Those that hadn't were lying about in soggy piles on the grass. There was a steady drizzle and the sky was heavy and grey. He thought of his estrangement and distance from his wife. Their lives had drifted so far apart over the last year. It had been nearly that long since they had made love. Did she have lovers? He thought then of his own and the sadness and pain that surrounded her.

"Damn, Draper!" he said out loud to the window. God, how he loathed the man!

There was a tentative knock at the door.

"Come in!" said Murdoch, feeling embarrassed.

Kevin opened the door and walked in. He looked around the office, as if expecting to see someone else present.

"Sorry to disturb you, Rich," began Kevin, but I was wondering if you were going to the reception tonight at Reading House."

"Oh that!" exclaimed Richard, "I had completely forgotten about it. - But yes I spoke to Margaret last weekend about it."

"I was just wondering how formal it was," said Kevin, with an anxious air, "And what time it started."

"Smart, but not evening wear and it starts at eight o'clock." replied Richard, forsaking the opportunity to tell Kevin to read the invitation properly.

"I had better tell Ella about it." said Kevin, "I forgot to mention it last night."

"You haven't told her, yet!" exclaimed Richard, "You're not really used to living with a woman - are you? It's all right for a man - you just pull your best suit out of the wardrobe, iron a decent shirt and polish your shoes. But for a woman there is the question of getting the right dress, the right shoes, the right jewellery."

"Maybe, I should ring her?" queried Kevin, tentatively.

"I think you should." replied Richard, with a smile. He could not help liking Kevin. He was so honest, open and simply naive.

"How did you get on yesterday with Draper?" asked Richard, deciding to take advantage of Kevin's innocence.

"It was awful - I mean that it was good in that Draper was really pleased with what we had done. But for the whole meeting Draper left a letter - of dismissal, I am sure - lying in front of me and then at the end he took it back and tore it up. I was nearly physically sick and I was so tired last night. I was in bed before eight o'clock. No wonder I forgot to tell Ella about the reception tonight."

"The man's a sadist," said Richard with real feeling. There was an unpleasant feeling in his stomach. He was sure that he knew who Draper's next victim would be - unless he did something about it.

"There was another knock on the door that Kevin had left half open and a clearly upset looking Sadie poked her head in.

"Sorry to disturb, you Dr Murdoch, but Professor Draper would like to see you immediately."

The formal titles and the distress in her face all pointed to one purpose for this summons. It was very tempting to say that he was too busy, but pointless. Richard braced himself and, apologising to an unenlightened Kevin, left.

He knocked on Draper's closed door and entered in response to a gruff summons.

He sat down, without waiting for an invitation, but Draper carried on reading the sheet in front of him and then picked up another one. Finally, after about a minute he looked up.

"Dr Murdoch," began Draper, in his clipped cold tone, "I have given you every opportunity to demonstrate your organisational abilities, what they are, with regard to the students and the timetabling, but this does not mean that I expected you to withdraw totally from research. I also had hoped that..."

The telephone rang. Draper stared at it with a look of pure hatred and then picked it up.

"Up yours," thought Murdoch to himself. "The silly bastard had forgotten to arrange to have his calls transferred to Sadie."

"This is not a good time." Draper said into the offending mouthpiece. Whoever it was persisted and Draper then looked up at Murdoch with almost a wary look.

"Hold on." He put his hand over the mouthpiece and then addressed Murdoch.

"We will have to continue our discussion on Monday. Sadie will inform you of the new time."

Taking this as a dismissal, Murdoch thankfully left the office. In the outer office Sadie looked up in surprise.

"Execution postponed," Murdoch said with a cryptic smile. Monday seemed a long way off and this gave him time to inform Ruth Hurley, the union rep, and prepare his defences.

DI Gareth Anderson munched on the last of his fig roll and then washed it down with the dregs of his coffee. He was a balding overweight man in his late thirties. His thin light brown hair had been combed over the receding hairline in a vain attempt to hide the bare scalp. His face was slightly puffy and his complexion was flushed. His dark jacket had scatterings of dandruff on the shoulders. His sharp blue eyes though were restless with an intelligent glint, which hinted at the man that lay behind them.

"Must cut back on these biscuits," he muttered to himself, half-heartedly.

It was late on Friday afternoon and, at last, he was getting some peace. He should really use the time to complete some of the never-ending paperwork. Instead he was taking the opportunity to read through again, DC Kent's slim sheet on a possible sighting of a Mantree Estate suspect. He had recognised the suspect's name this morning when he first read the report. He had after all interviewed her on Tuesday, as the victim of a break in and what looked like an attempted repeat of the assault on the Silverman woman.

There was certainly something inadequate, to say the least about her story of what she had been doing before coming to Bristol. He had let it go on Tuesday, as it seemed to have nothing to do with the break-in. Kent's report was brief, but she clearly voiced her surprise that she was not the suspect. Thinking about the woman that he had interviewed Gareth was surprised as well. She fitted the description perfectly. He felt slightly guilty that he had not made the connection himself. His musings were interrupted by the phone. It was the desk sergeant saying that Manchester CID wanted to talk to him.

"This is DI Wilkins here," the phone squawked, "I want to talk to you about the possible Mantree Estate suspect that you reported."

"What a coincidence," replied Anderson, "I am just looking at the report of the sighting from last night. As luck would have it, I have already interviewed this woman over another matter and to be blunt the match with the description is very good."

"That what I wanted to talk to you about," said Wilkins, "We have found parts of the pelvis of the second body and it is definitely male. We have found no evidence of a third body so the woman is still missing. There have been several reports of sightings from around the country, but yours is one of the most promising. Do you think that it would be possible to pull this woman in to establish her identity?"

"It should be." responded Anderson, "We know exactly where she is living. I should be able to get someone there within the hour."

After completing the call, Anderson put the phone down. DC Kent had already started her shift. He would go himself and take her along. He was already getting up from his chair when the desk sergeant came in.

"Sorry, sir!" he began apologetically, "But there's been trouble on Doncaster Road and someone's been stabbed. Don't know how serious yet."

Ella stared unhappily into the full-length mirror on the door of the dark wooden wardrobe. She had put on her other dress, the one she had brought from the charity shop for going out. It was dark blue with white frills and a white frilly collar. It buttoned up to the neck. On someone with delicate features like Paul's Fiona, it would have been perfect, creating a demure modest effect. But with her broad pale face and nose and full lips, it simply looked ridiculous. She looked like a clown.

She would have to put the low cut, maroon dress on. The trouble was it would make her look like a tart. Still better that than to look like a figure of fun.

"Ella! Are you nearly ready? The taxi will be here in ten minutes." Kevin's anxious voice floated up the stairs.

Ella looked at the little digital alarm clock on the bedside table. Five past seven, Kevin was right. It was his fault she thought to herself. He had only told her when he got home. He said that he had meant to phone, but had forgotten after becoming immersed with Douglas Grant in their project.

Ella unbuttoned the blue dress and threw it on to the bed. She opened the wardrobe and took out the maroon dress and quickly pulled it over her head. She put her arms through the short sleeves and smoothed it into place. That did look a lot better, she thought, but it certainly highlighted her cleavage and the swell of her breasts.

"The taxis here," called Kevin, in a panicky voice.

"Be down in a minute, love." responded Ella, calmly, "Just ask him to wait."

Ella gave her anarchic hair a cursory comb and then pulled on a thin white, woollen shawl. She felt much happier. Tonight was going to be hard enough without having to worry about her appearance.

Her mind then passed on to the reception. She had been in such a rush that she had not had much time to worry about it. It would be difficult though - a lot of intellectual well-read and well-informed men and women. At least she had done some reading. Rules of engagement she thought. Do not drink too much and keep her answers short and succinct. If she felt that she was getting over-excited in her speech or going on too long then simply stop.

"Ella!" shouted Kevin's voice, now clearly in total panic, "The taxi's blocking the road and someone's coming."

"OK, love," replied Ella, "I'm coming."

As she came out the house she saw that Kevin was right. A car was waiting behind the taxi and as she looked she saw the lights of yet another car turning into the street. The evening was cold and she felt a bit under-dressed, but at least it was dry.

"Terribly sorry," she said climbing into the taxi, beside Kevin.

"No problem," replied the taxi driver, laconically, as he engaged first gear and pulled away, "It's not me who is being held up."

DI Gareth Anderson was feeling extremely frustrated. The Doncaster Road incident had turned out to be more minor than initial reports indicated, but it had cost him an hour and a half. Now within a few yards of his goal he was thwarted by what appeared to be a taxi parked in the middle of the incredibly narrow street with a large Volvo estate already stuck behind it.

"Thank God for that!" he exclaimed to DC Jane Kent, as the taxi pulled away, just as they were coming up behind the Volvo. The Volvo moved off as well and drove to the far end of the street where it parked. Jane Kent stopped the car outside Kevin's house.

"I don't see a parking place." She said to Gareth.

"Oh, just park in the middle of the street and put the blue light on." responded a clearly exasperated DI.

They got out and walked up to Kevin's door. Gareth Anderson knocked and, with no answer after about a minute, knocked again.

CHAPTER 16

The taxi stopped right in front of the entrance of the George Reading House. Ella looked out of the window of the taxi at it. The building was a two-storey structure, consisting of two wings arranged in a 'V' shape. They were inside the 'V' at its apex, where, instead of a sharp junction of the two wings, there was a flat wall consisting mainly of the four glass doors of the entrance. Through the doors was a well-lit reception area with a counter immediately opposite the doors, where two porters were obviously registering visitors and taking coats. Behind the counter was an ample cloakroom. Two staircases swept up to the upper floor.

Because the wings were at an acute angle to each other they partially enfolded the entrance area. To Ella's right, the wing was in total darkness, but to her left the upper floor blazed with light. This was obviously where the reception was being held. Each wing must have been over 100 feet in length. The left wing was lined both top and bottom with windows and it was from these upper windows that the bright light shone. However, only the first half of the right hand wing had windows the outer half showed only its plain brick surface, broken only just below the roof, where there was a series of long windows no more than a foot high.

Ella opened the door of the taxi and stepped out into the night. It was cold. Even the bright lights at the entrance and the well-lit car park, just beyond the dark right hand wing, could not obscure the brightest stars in the very clear sky. Kevin paid the taxi driver and joined Ella. He was blinking and looking a little disorientated.

"Come on!" said Ella, "Let's go and have fun."

On entering the bright reception area, they joined the queue for the cloakroom. Kevin had an outer jacket that he wanted to hand in and Ella thought that she may as well get rid of the woollen shawl. In addition, Kevin would have to sign Ella in. There were two couples in front of them that Ella did not recognise and neither, apparently, did Kevin.

Ella studied them carefully, but unobtrusively. The two women wore smart evening dresses, which made hers appear quite shabby. Their shoes were specially designed for eveningwear, being totally impractical for anything else, with their high heels and silvered appearance. Ella's, on the other hand, were meant to be worn outside and hence appeared chunky by comparison.

One of the couples looked remarkably young, no more than their early twenties. They both looked a bit apprehensive and shy. The other couple was much older, probably in their middle fifties. They were the complete opposite appearing confident and relaxed.

After Kevin had signed her in, they ascended the sweeping left-hand staircase together, Ella tucking her arm into Kevin's. At the top, they saw ahead of them a double door that was propped open and beyond the bright lights of the large ballroom itself.

The ballroom was less than a quarter full, but they were quite early so it would probably fill up more. It had a relatively high ceiling. Ella estimated it to be about fifteen feet high. At the far end, she could see two doors and as she watched a smartly dressed waitress in a white blouse, black skirt and white frilly pinny came out carrying a tray laden with filled wine glasses, some containing white wine and some red. She noticed that there was another, similarly dressed waitress moving about the room, offering wine. To the right hand side towards the back was a long table loaded with a buffet and a smaller table next to it covered in more filled wineglasses. The two tables were completely covered with white tablecloths.

To Ella the scene seemed like something out of a fairy tale. The glamour, the elegance, the sheer sumptuousness of it was both thrilling and stimulating. She had to be careful. She could easily get overexcited and talk too much. She looked at Kevin. If she found the environment strange, but intoxicating, then poor Kevin was finding it forbidding. He looked distinctly unhappy and worried.

"Oh!" she said, encouragingly, taking his arm "Isn't this exciting?"

"Yes, I suppose so." said Kevin, who did not sound particularly convinced.

Ella slowly moved them towards the buffet table. She was quite keen to try the food and, already, some people were filling paper plates, so it was clearly not out of order to start helping oneself.

"Kevin!" a voice suddenly called, just before Ella had achieved her objective.

Ella turned to see a man of about six feet coming towards them. He had extremely thin red hair and freckles. Although she estimated his age at about fifty, he looked fit and healthy. With him was a similarly aged woman who was even slightly taller. She was dressed simply in a long, pink skirt with a separate white blouse, stretched over large breasts. She was not overweight though and like her husband looked fit. Despite the plainness of her outfit, Ella thought that it suited her.

"Dr Sullivan - Jack" stammered Kevin, struggling to find the right form of address, "It's good to see you."

"I think you have already met Hilda," responded Dr Sullivan, indicating the tall woman next to him.

"And you must be the mysterious Ella," said Jack Sullivan, after a short pause in which he had waited in vain for Kevin to introduce her. Ella looked into the light blue eyes that had turned towards her and shook the offered hand. It was worrying to think of people that she had not even met discussing and wondering about her.

"That's me," she said brightly, "It's a pleasure to meet you."

"I understand from Richard Murdoch that you and Kevin met under very unusual circumstances." said Jack Sullivan, giving Ella a quizzical look.

"They certainly were," responded Ella, smoothly.

"If it had not been for Kevin I do not know where I would be. He quite simply rescued me, not only from a possible immediate death from exposure, but also from the whole dreadful environment that I lived in." She held Kevin's arm and gave him a smile.

"I can imagine," said Jack, "Both Hilda and myself were brought up in Bedminster, which was quite a poor working class estate in Bristol. Our families were poor, but most of us had hope. Nowadays on the large estates there seems precious little of that. In my day, there were skilled jobs. Now the more employable ones get jobs in supermarkets and the rest..." trailing off, he held his hands out in despair.

Jack went on to explain how he had failed his eleven plus, but had gained qualifications on day release at a local factory and had been sponsored for a fulltime university engineering course.

"No employer would do that now," he finished, sadly.

Hilda was equally forthcoming and briefly told of her work as a secretary for a local solicitor.

Ella enjoyed their company, they were more natural than she had expected the people here to be, though Jack Sullivan at times displayed the presence of an almost ferocious intelligence and a distinct inability to appreciate that not everyone shared it.

After ten minutes, the Sullivans made their excuses and left to talk to another couple. Ella tried to restart their slow movement to the buffet table, but they had barely gone two steps when a loud clipped voice boomed out.

"Dr Hansen, glad you could make it."

Ella felt Kevin's arm noticeably stiffen in hers. She looked in the direction of the voice. Coming towards them was a stocky bull of a man, but only about Ella's height with close-cropped hair. A small woman, with her head down, trailed behind him.

"Professor Draper." stuttered Kevin.

"I've been looking at my notes from our meeting yesterday. The work you and Douglas did looks even better than it did then. Well done!"

"Thank you" Kevin replied, almost inaudibly.

"And you must be Ella," said Draper turning, with a beaming smile, to her. His eyes wandering to her exposed cleavage.

"I believe that you should be congratulated as well, as without you it probably would never have happened."

"Perhaps, but I certainly didn't play any part in the work itself," she replied modestly, with a laugh.

Draper smiled broadly.

"And where are you from?" he asked, "It sounds like you're from my neck of the woods."

"Manchester, the Pallings estate."

"Ah yes!" said Draper, "My father used to own a wine merchants on the Mantree estate next door. I'm sorry, but that was an awful place. He had to shut it down. There was very little business, but everyone trying to steal."

"That dreadful killing there did not surprise me. When I was up there I met that poor young man. He came to our church to give a talk. Very committed! Very brave!"

Ella was stunned to silence. Her cheeks burned.

"And, of course, it has caused ... Oh excuse me, but I must just catch Professor Travers."

It was with considerable relief that Ella saw Draper rushing off to speak to a small elderly man. The wife was still in tow. She was even shorter than Draper. She was possibly quite pretty, but with her bowed head, she seemed to be continuously studying the floor.

"Was that his wife?" Ella asked Kevin, partly to divert him from Draper's comments, but also because she was genuinely curious. "It was strange that he never introduced us."

"Yes, I think so," replied Kevin, vaguely, "I have only seen her once before myself."

"I suppose that it must be very difficult being married to someone like Draper," said Ella, "He has a very forceful personality."

As she spoke she became conscious of a drop in volume of the general hubbub around her, which had been growing until now as more guests had arrived. She also noticed that Kevin was no longer looking at her, but instead was looking over her left shoulder towards the entrance door of the reception room.

She turned herself, curious to see what the attraction was.   The

Murdochs had just arrived.

Richard Murdoch was dressed in a smart, dark-grey suit with a white shirt and dark tie, but it was not him who was attracting attention. It was the woman with him.

She was dressed in a sheer plain cream coloured dress that hugged her curves. Although it looked simple, it fitted to maximum effect and Ella suspected that it was far from cheap. But it was the person who wore it that really made it. She had a narrow waist that swept out to her well-proportioned hips below and to her breasts above. The breasts were full, but not over large. The dress fitted to the base of her pale-brown neck, round which was a simple black choker. Her face was oval, with a delicate nose and a hint of freckles. Otherwise it was unblemished. Her blond hair was cut into a fringe at the front, while the rest swayed just above the shoulders.

The whole effect was stunning and Ella became conscious of her own thick waist and inappropriate bulges. She became aware too of the other women in the room, whom just moments before, had seemed so beautiful and elegant. Now their art was revealed, paint, make-up, tight underwear, padded bras. All was now of no avail. Not when faced with the genuine article.

"Not a women's woman," thought Ella, noticing that Kevin was still staring.

The goddess that was the only word to describe her glided across the room, with her husband moving easily beside her. There was no doubt that they presented an extremely handsome couple and they were coming towards her and Kevin.

"Good evening," said Richard, as he came up to them, "I would like to introduce my wife Margaret - and Margaret this is Kevin, whom I think you know - and this is the amazing Ella, whom I told you so much about."

With this last phrase, Richard turned towards Ella and flashed a particularly warm smile.

Ella took Margaret's hand. The hand was cool and dry. Margaret smiled, somewhat automatically, at Ella.

"Richard has indeed told me a great deal about you. It is certainly a pleasure to meet you at last." Margaret's voice had a pleasing huskiness and she gave a full smile revealing a set of perfect teeth. Her eyes were golden and seemed to be scrutinising Ella.

"And it's a great pleasure to meet you, Richard has told me much about you" replied Ella wondering how to gauge her reply.

"We hoped to be here earlier," continued Margaret, "But that young girl who baby-sits for us was late again. I really think that we should try to get someone else."

"Oh don't be harsh on her, dear," countered Richard, "Her mother would drive any offspring to distraction."

"I suppose so," said Margaret, "Ella have you been to Bristol before and how are you finding it?"

"It's my first time here," responded Ella, "And I find it really nice. I especially like Gloucester Road. It's so old-fashioned and there are so many interesting shops."

"There are indeed," said Margaret, "I was born in Bristol and have always found it beautiful. It is let down though by the low standard of its education. Did you know that education in Bristol is even worse than that in Islington?"

"Oh dear!" Ella exclaimed, not quite sure how to respond.

"I had to go to one of their corporation schools here and it was truly awful. I hated every minute. Fortunately, daddy was eventually able to get me into a private school. It is so important that our girls never have to endure what I did."

"Richard has told me that you have two delightful young girls."

"Yes, indeed. That's why it's so important that they don't get ruined at the wrong school." Margaret continued, ignoring the attempt to divert her.

"Now dear," intervened Richard, "I am sure that Ella and Kevin don't want to hear all our worries."

"You just don't take it seriously, do you?" Margaret glared at her husband, "You have no idea what it was like!"

Ella noted that even in anger Margaret was beautiful, perhaps even more so.

"I can understand you," said Ella, boldly trying to calm her, "The school I went to in Manchester was terrible and there were some dreadful people there - even the girls. I knew one who was suspended twice for injuring other pupils in fights." Ella failed to point out that the miscreant was herself.

Margaret smiled at Ella for her support.

"I am sorry, though." she added, "I do go on a bit, but it is so important to me."

Ella noted that Margaret's upper lip was quivering slightly from the emotion.

"I still have a lot of Bristol to see," said Ella, again trying to divert Margaret, "How long have you lived here?"

"About six years." answered Richard, "We moved down here after I finished my post-doc at Durham. I must say though I do miss Durham that is a really beautiful city, though very much dominated by the University, which you don't find to be the case in Bristol because it is so much bigger."

Ella noticed that Margaret was looking at someone on the other side of the buffet table. It was Mrs Draper now staring at a plate in her hand and nibbling at a sandwich.

"You must excuse me," said Margaret, "I really must go and cheer her up."

Ella watched her walk over to Mrs Draper and speak to her. The poor woman did not even look up.

"Terrible!" said Richard in a hissed whisper to Ella and Kevin, "That poor woman really suffers with that brute. Most people would treat a dog better. Margaret does her best to cheer her up when she gets the chance, which unfortunately is not very often. He married her for her money. Apparently her father owned a grocery chain. She would have been better off poor."

Usually a remark, like Richard's last one would have annoyed Ella. After all she was born poor and hated it. But she could see what he meant in this case. From her appearance Mrs Draper's spirit was completely broken and once that was gone there was nothing. She had wondered why Draper had married such a woman. She would have thought that someone like Margaret would have been much more his type - a woman who would advertise his success, who made other men envious. But now she knew.

"Where is your illustrious colleague, Kevin?" asked Richard, in a more normal voice.

For a moment Kevin just looked baffled.

"Oh you mean Doug, I don't know; he had said that he and Karen were coming, but it is getting late"

Ella saw Kevin's eyes glance to a clock mounted high on the opposite wall. The hands were at half past eight.

"Half past eight!" Douglas Grant looked up from his watch to see the taxi's red tail lights disappearing down the drive away from Reading house.

"We're very late," he said to Karen, not attempting to hide his impatience.

Karen stood beside him in a flower-patterned dress and a grey wrap. She seemed impervious to the cold and made no response to Douglas' clear impatience. Her face held that dull apathetic look that it had held all week and which was driving Douglas to anger. He had arrived at her house in good time, but she had not even started to get ready. By the time he had cajoled her into activity and she had dressed herself, they were an hour later than he had intended.

Perhaps she was brooding over the fact that he had not yet gone to the police. But he thought not. She had been quietly chivvying him on that, but now she never mentioned it. It was more as if she had lost interest in everything.

They entered one of the glass doors into the now empty foyer. Only one porter was present to sign in the stragglers and take their coats.

Having handed in his coat, Douglas took Karen's arm and led her up the stairway.

Margaret watched Sally Draper walk away from her towards the exit. She had upset Sally, but that was not hard to do. She was still recovering herself. It had been silly to get so agitated in front of Kevin and the strange Ella, but Richard did not understand. And how could he, she had not told him. She still remembered that fateful day.

She had allowed Sean the school wide-boy to take her to his home. She had half-believed his protestations of good intent, but half not wanted to believe them. She remembered her feeling of excitement. I won't stay long she had said to herself, but she had not meant it. He was both persuasive and sexually precocious, but the worst thing was it was what she had wanted; or allowed him to do.

She still remembered that small bedroom in that dilapidated council house; the fading aeroplane pictures from an earlier phase of boyhood and the newer pictures of heavy metal bands, the dirty bed with its soiled linen. He had taken her there, the stuck-up beautiful bitch. She had hated it. Felt dirtied by it, but also excited. The very submission had excited her. It was rape of a sort, but of the soul. Then his friend had called. Found them together.

She had bathed several times that evening and the following day, but she never felt completely clean again. At school, life became unbearable. Perhaps if his friend had not called? Perhaps if she had left then? But no, it was soon round the whole school, the beautiful stuck-up bitch was a slag. Sean saw his conquest as a way of raising his status and boasted to the others, while treating her with harsh contempt. The boys were bad with their sniggering and half-hopeful lewd requests, but the girls were much worse. She was bottom of the social heap at a bottom school.

She had almost gone under and then poor fat Jean, smelly Jean, lardy Jean, pork Jean, had hung herself in her bedroom. There was no remorse from her tormentors. When you're fifteen driving someone to suicide was a success. Margaret had found the strength then. She was not going to give them the pleasure.

A few months later her father's business had improved and he had got her back into a private school, but it was too late she could never be at ease with herself again. She thought then of her little girls, thought of their lives being blighted as hers had been.

As Douglas and Karen entered the reception room, Sally Draper brushed past hurrying out and across the landing to the toilets. Karen looked after her and then unhooked her arm from his.

"Go on in yourself, I am afraid I need to go to the toilet."

Before Douglas could respond, she was gone and he was left to enter the reception room alone. His sense of unease was increasing. He knew where it was coming from and he had really needed Karen to be with him. He had only seen Kevin's mystery woman once; a brief glimpse from the back as she had gone down the stairs from Kevin's office on Kevin's first day back. But that incredibly fair, frizzy, splayed hair stuck in his mind. It reminded him of another woman. Same height, but thinner, in a short tarty skirt looking on in horror as he and Mark gave her three male gangster friends a painful demonstration of their martial arts skills. One day later the mobsters took their terrible revenge.

At first he had dismissed it, but he found that he could never ask Kevin for details of how they had met. Gradually, he picked up second-hand some of the story. Richard Murdoch had the original version, but he and Richard rarely spoke. He knew that they had met somewhere near Manchester and his disquiet had increased. It had to be just a coincidence. He had seen her die, tumbling backwards into the black abyss.

But the stories of his foster uncle would spring to mind. The man had a much more primitive religion that his evangelical relatives. For him the world was peopled by demons and evil spirits. One tale he remembered in particular was how an avenging spirit would take possession of the body of a murder victim and go and seek vengeance on the perpetrator. You tell by the eyes, he had said. The rest looks as in life, but the eyes give it away and reveal the supernatural power within. On this his foster uncle had rolled his own eyes to great effect. He and Mark listening, with the confidence of twelve year old boys, would laugh nervously, the doubt remaining.

And who was to say he was wrong. Perhaps Christianity, even mathematics, were mere desperate, constructs of a complex, but incredibly fragile, civilisation, which existed precariously surrounded by a dark chaos of malignant forces.

Douglas shook himself. He was feeling the strain and had to get a grip.

He walked forward into the room and glanced around. At the far end of the buffet table he caught sight of Richard Murdoch and Kevin and, facing them, with her back to him, the mysterious woman with the distinctive very fair curly hair.

Doug began walking towards them. He had to lay this ghost. At any moment, she would turn around showing a different face, a different person.

He was only a few steps away when Richard finally noticed him. He said something to Kevin and the woman. Kevin glanced up and smiled. The woman began to turn.

The flat broad face and nose, the freckles, he searched desperately for a difference - the prominent birthmark above the left eyebrow. But the eyes, they were different. He remembered them as cloudy, indistinct. Now they were icy piercing daggers that stabbed into his. He registered, as from a long distance, the rest of the face breaking into a horrified recognition, even despair. But the eyes never wavered, the rest was facsimile; it was the eyes that told what was truly there.

Douglas staggered backwards, almost shouting in terror. There was a crash as he banged into a waitress behind him, the full wineglasses on her laden tray, scattering noisily and smashing on the floor. His balance went and he went over too distraught to react properly. There was a sharp pain in his face and then his head hit the floor and blackness engulfed him.

Kevin stared. His mouth hung open his posture frozen. Somewhere a voice said, "He must be having a fit". Douglas lay motionless on the floor amid the broken glasses and spilt wine, blood flowing from a cut on his cheek. Behind him the young waitress, deathly white, was still holding her now empty tray, her face transfixed with horror. It was like a frozen tableau, as if the film had been stopped. And then into the picture stepped two tall figures, the Sullivans. Hilda bent down to Douglas Grant's motionless body; Jack spoke in a loud authoritative voice.

"Everyone get back! Give him air! Any trained medics in the room!"

A woman in her forties came forward and bent down with Hilda to examine Grant.

Kevin became aware of his mouth hanging open and closed it.

"What had happened?"

He had glanced up, when Richard had motioned to him and seen Douglas only a few steps away. He had thought that he had looked a bit pale and even anxious, but he had not expected what had come next. The look of sheer terror that had come into Douglas's face, the staggering backwards, the smashing of the wineglasses and then his clumsy fall to the floor and the audible bang of his head. He turned to his companions, but both Richard and Ella had disappeared.

Douglas was slowly getting to his feet helped by the two women supporting him. He looked groggy, but his eyes seemed to be wildly searching the room for someone, a look of fear on his face.

His eyes met Kevin's and the look of fear turned to anger. Catching the two women supporting him by surprise, he broke free of them and advanced on Kevin.

"You!" he screamed, "You brought her - that thing - here. Did you never think to question who or what she really was? She is the one who killed Mark!"

The last sentence was shouted with Douglas's face now only a foot away from Kevin's, blood streaming down from his left cheek, the eyes rolling wildly.

"Come on old man, let's get you to Casualty," said the calm authoritative voice of Jack Sullivan, as he and his wife took one side each of Grant and turned him towards the door. However Grant's strength was now clearly all gone, he visibly sagged between his two supporters as they led him to the door. The three left, followed by the other woman who had helped.

Kevin felt nauseous. Everyone was looking at him. He knew that a physical reaction was setting in. He had to get to the toilet. Fortunately, no one tried to stop him leaving.

Ella sat in the gloom on the hard, plastic cafeteria chair, staring out into the nearly total blackness of the gymnasium below.

She had left the reception room, as soon as Grant had fallen; nearly blindly crossed the landing past the toilets and into the darkened cafeteria on the opposite side of the stairs in the other wing of Reading House. The door to the cafeteria had been closed but not locked. It was dimly lit only by the light coming through the glass panelling from the illuminated landing. At the far end of the cafeteria was a glass wall from where one could look out into the gymnasium below. There was also a stair case at this far end, where one could descend from the cafeteria to the floor below taking one directly to the changing rooms and the gymnasium. It would also provide an additional means of escape in the event of a fire.

She had realised that this would probably provide a means of leaving the building unobserved via a ground floor fire exit. But she had not taken it. Instead she had turned to her left and sat at this table behind a column, in the shadows. She had heard the door of the cafeteria open and close again. Someone had followed her. But, whoever it was had crossed the cafeteria and went straight down the stairs. After all that was where she should have gone.

She had not, because suddenly she had decided that she did not want to run anymore. She was under no illusions. If one confessed to a crime and was contrite, one usually got out of jail sooner, but also one tended to be charged with every offence covered by one's confession and thus to receive an initial longer sentence. She thought of herself and Kevin and the tears came to her eyes. He would run a mile. She heard the door of the cafeteria open and close again and other footsteps cross the floor and pass down the stairs; probably a woman this time from the sound of them.

Fate had certainly dealt her a funny hand. She had immediately recognised Douglas as a close friend of their victim. She had expected an angry denunciation. The terror and panic that actually occurred was inexplicable. Perhaps he thought that she was still carrying a gun. She remembered how almost casually he had brushed aside Johnny's knife and disarmed him. It just did not make sense.

However, it had provided her an opportunity to escape and here she was squandering it. She wiped the tears from her eyes and got up. She would go back - no more running.

At that moment there was a loud retort from the direction of the stairs. She turned to it in bafflement and then came a second. In her mind's eye a young man was sinking to the ground, staring in horror at the blood pouring from stomach wounds.

She hurried to the stairs and went down the steps. The stairs curved halfway round before reaching the bottom and exited into a dimly lit passage. To her left, just two or three yards away was a double door at the end of the passage that clearly led to the gym. From the other direction she thought that she heard a sound. It was a gentle rushing sound like an untuned radio or a shower. She turned to her right and walked a few paces along the passage. There were two closed doors on each side, marked private. Ella guessed that they probably contained equipment for the gym. Further on were two more doors. The one to her right was closed and marked "Ladies changing rooms", the other though was open and bright light spilled from it. It was from here that the sound of the shower was coming.

She hesitated slightly. Was a man having a shower at this time? She walked in.

In the bright light she could see wooden slatted benches ranged against two walls and above them were empty clothes hooks. The third wall had three rows of lockers fitted to it and the fourth gave a wide entrance to shower stalls and toilets beyond. The exposed walls were finished with a speckled, fawn stone effect plaster. The whole room had a clean fresh, look about it, but the smell of male sweat still clung strongly to it.

Ella cautiously walked through the wide entrance to the shower stalls. The noise of spraying water was coming from the furthest one of the three. She stepped into the shower room and walked past the other two stalls until she could see directly into the third.

Draper was slumped down in the stall, his glazed open eyes staring sightlessly at her. He was fully dressed, the water spraying on to his face and body. There was a hole in his forehead and behind his head on the wall a bloody mess of bone and brain where the bullet had taken the back of his head off. In his chest was a three-inch wide circle of blood where the other bullet had gone.

Ella stepped back, involuntarily. She was used to messy death, but this was unexpected. As she did so her heel kicked something metallic and hard. She turned to look and froze in total disbelief and horror. Lying on the floor behind her was a small handgun. But not any gun. The damaged hand grip, the clay stains, the spilt nail varnish on the lower barrel. This was her gun. It should be back at Kevin's house under her bed in the spare room where she kept it in a shoebox with spare ammunition. It simply couldn't be. She picked it up and looked at it. There was no doubt - it was hers.

There was a noise behind her. She turned around. Facing her was one of the porters. His age-lined face deathly white, as he stared in visible fear at the weapon in her hand. Others were crowding into the changing room behind him. She recognised Margaret Murdoch, Sally Draper, Karen Reading another couple she had seen earlier upstairs and, just coming through the door, Kevin.

"I'm afraid that it is Professor Draper, someone has shot him." she said, returning the gun to the floor.

There was a gasp from Sally Draper and she came slowly forward. She took one glance at her husband's body, put her hand to her mouth and hurried from the room, without another sound. Margaret Murdoch turned to follow her.

Everyone else just stared at Ella with accusing eyes.

Before anyone could find anything appropriate to say, there was a commotion at the door and the wild figure of Douglas Grant with a makeshift bandage on his face, stained in blood burst in. He was closely followed by the tall figure of Hilda Sullivan, who was vainly trying to restrain him. He rushed passed the others and stared into the shower stall. He turned on Ella then.

"Murderess!" he screamed, "Can't you stop killing? I thought that you had come back for me."

Faced with this violent, insane rage Ella backed against the wall and raised her hands to ward off the expected blows.

"Douglas, stop it!" screamed the voice of Karen Reading, "Let the police deal with her. Haven't you already done enough harm?"

Diverted he turned from Ella, but his rage was not completely spent. Seeing Kevin by the door, he shouted at him.

"You weak-minded fool; you let that demon in! Look at what she has done now! Come on look!"

For a moment, Ella thought that Grant would drag poor Kevin to the shower stall and force him to look, but, suddenly his strength was gone again, and he let Karen and Hilda take him away.

Ella looked at Kevin, but he avoided her eyes. He looked pale, sick and near tears. There was no doubt that Grant's attack on him had struck home. After all Ella admitted to herself, it was partially true, but not completely. Her heart ached. She felt like crying herself.

CHAPTER 17

Richard Murdoch shut the door of his two year old Ford Focus and looked around the small car park next to the Mathematics building. Usually, during the week it was full of cars and, he often had to park in the larger car park next to the Chemistry building, but at half past eight on a Saturday morning he had it nearly all to himself. There was only one other car in it - a small red sports car that seemed familiar. He shielded his eyes from the low bright sun, which even at half past eight on an autumn morning was warm. It was the promise of a great day and it was indeed a great day with the prospects of many more to come.

His eyes scanned the sporadic nearly bare trees set in the shorn grass of the campus and turned towards the low, two-storey, brick structure of the Mathematics department - his Mathematics department. Draper was dead. It was hard to be charitable about the man and he was not going to try. It still puzzled him that Draper had put him second in command. It was only nominal, of course, but Draper's death had given it a much greater significance. Could he hold on to it? As far as he knew, there was no one else who coveted the job.

He unlocked the glass doors to his department and walked in. He went past the small, wooden porter's box and up the stairs. His footsteps echoed on the concrete steps. He felt like he was in an extremely pleasant dream - almost a sexual ecstasy.

At the thought of sex, his mind turned to Margaret - and Aggie. Margaret was the illusion that he and all men desired. He had married her, but he felt that he had got no closer to her than those male legions that had enviously seen them together. Even when the physical side of their marriage had existed, she had seemed disengaged. Now it was only the girls who held them together.

He thought then of her perfect body and briefly envied his past self.

Ultimately, in a relationship he needed warmth, affection and love. Poor Margaret, he thought, she seemed to have none to offer, except to the girls. To them she was different. Her love for them was deep and she treated them with a great gentleness, but did not spoil them. Yes, there was a fine loving side to Margaret, but he could not reach it. Or she would not let him.

Aggie on the other hand was the complete opposite - overweight, ill-proportioned, small asymmetric breasts, a big nose, cellulite. But an inner warmth that made his heart lift when he saw her. Her wide mouth would break into a genuine, welcoming grin. She would kiss him with unrestrained passion. He would put his arms around her, feeling the sensuous folds of flesh at her waist. Aggie looked a mess, but made a wonderful lover.

He had managed to see her yesterday. She was much better and seemed to be recovering, getting her strength back. Soon she would be out of hospital and back home. His fists clenched and unclenched at the thought of what had been done to her. It had proved one thing though. He really was in love with her.

He and Margaret had not made love (copulated would be a better word) for nearly 18 months. He would have to speak to her. Come to an understanding to maintain the shell of their marriage until the girls had left home. He wondered if Margaret had lovers. She was out often enough. But it did not really matter anymore.

He found himself outside the door of Draper's office - Draper's former office- now his. He walked into the outer office and glanced at Sadie's desk and PC. She was on his side and would help him through the administrative jungle that he would face. He then turned and opened the door of Draper's main office. He looked at the long table and his eyes travelled along it to the oak desk at the end - his desk. He had no feeling of expecting Draper to still be there, so it came as a shock to see a figure sitting exactly where Draper should be. It was bent forward in the chair looking in one of the desk drawers. Small hands pulled out a dark, A4 desk diary and put it on the desk and froze. He found himself staring into the pale, blue eyes of Karen Reading. She blushed a deep red and her mouth opened, but nothing came out.

Richard carried on looking at her.

"Caught red-handed or at least red-faced." he finally said, his sense of humour getting the better of him.

"I presume you have an explanation for going through what is now my desk."

"I was just checking for an appointment that Doug was concerned about. He is really not well enough to come himself." Her poise had partly returned. "I'm sorry, I really should have checked with you."

Her posh, honeyed accent, the product of endless hours of elocution lessons, irritated Richard, but he decided to be civil. He disliked Grant and, unfairly, by association his fiancé. But he also knew that Grant was one of the best assets the department had. He would somehow have to mend his fences with Grant and also get him to again work with Kevin. That would be two major tasks.

"No problem." he responded to her, struggling to keep the sarcasm out of his voice, "Would you like a cup of tea or coffee."

"No, no thank you." she answered, "I've got to go now. I promised Doug that I would be round at his place early."

She picked up her handbag and, with a perfunctory farewell, rushed out the door. Richard's eyes wandered back to the desk diary, which lay unopened on the desk. As they did so something else caught his eye. A piece of paper was hanging out one of the filing cabinets. It had been jammed in the door when someone had carelessly or hurriedly shut it. Not the sort of thing that Sadie or the late Professor would do. Had she being going through the whole office?

He walked around the desk and sat down. Only the desk diary was on it. He opened it up curiously and looked at what was on next week. Very little by the looks of it, he saw with relief. The Friday had a slightly strange entry, "Take afternoon off for extra shopping" and below it in pencil a firmly written "cancelled".

Richard shut the diary. Sadie would draw his attention to what needed to be attended to. He looked up from the desk to the long table. A Draper's eye view of where his victims had sat.

His mind meandered around the issues that he would face and settled on the question of Grant and Hansen. There was no doubt that this partnership was extremely creative. But how could it be restored when Kevin had brought the blessed Mark's murderer to Bristol, who had then proceeded to kill the beloved leader.

He thought then of Ella. He liked her. As far as he was concerned she had brought nothing, but good fortune, but that was, of course, an extremely personal view.

CHAPTER 18

"Emma Barnes - alias Ella Slater," thought DI Gareth Anderson, angrily turning over the names in his mind.

He found it very hard not to hate her. She had made a complete fool of him. Twice he had failed to arrest her and the second time had resulted in her carrying out a particularly blatant murder. He had to stay calm. Last night during the interrogation he had caught himself losing his temper. He had to try and remain more objective.

He looked up from his coffee into the cool appraising, brown eyes of DI George Wilkins. He was surprisingly young, only in his early thirties, tall and slender with a prominent nose. He had an annoying laconic, but analytical manner, which was reinforced by his Yorkshire accent. Although the man had driven down from Manchester in the early hours of the morning and had still not slept, he looked fresh and alert.

Gareth Anderson made a mental note not to underestimate him. This was a big deal for the Manchester police. They had had a lot of bad publicity over their initial handling of this case. There was no doubt that, despite his youth, his superiors saw Wilkins as a very capable, safe pair of hands.

"Douglas Grant was the foster brother of Mark Ashton, the young man who was murdered," said Wilkins, "Anything that he feels he must tell us could be most interesting."

Gareth felt frustrated. He was eager to charge Barnes, but he really should wait for the forensics. It was ten o'clock now, but they would not have any results until after lunch. Nor, could he imagine what useful information Dr Grant would have. However, he did feel curious; the man was so desperate to talk to them.

There was a short knock on the door of the interview room and DC Kent ushered in a young couple. They both looked shockingly ill. The man had a bandage around his head and a large plaster on his left cheek. His physique looked like it had once been athletic, but now his shoulders were hunched and he carried himself awkwardly. If anything the woman looked even worse. Her expression was glazed and frozen, as if afraid to let some great internal pain show itself. The red rims around her pale blue, watery eyes gave it away though.

"Now are you sure that you would not like a solicitor present?" asked Gareth.

"No, as long as Karen can stay" Grant replied, in a quiet voice, putting his hand on the knee of the woman beside him, who struggled to return an encouraging smile.

Gareth went through the preliminaries and started the cassette tape and then he, Wilkins and DC Kent who was sitting, unobtrusively, on a chair against the wall all turned expectantly to Grant.

Grant began to speak and, as he spoke, those dreadful days became like the present. He felt like he was living them again.

The sky was an absolute azure blue. The late afternoon, September sun shone down on the maisonettes, battered semi-detacheds and boarded up, steel shuttered shops of the Mantree Estate, the series of three high rise buildings rose to their modest height. Douglas looked out over it all from the high ground in its litter-strewn park, soon he would return to Bristol. He had escaped. It was thanks to Mark and his family. They had taken him in, cared for him and loved him as one of their own.

They had a different skin colour from him and a religion that he did not share, but they had taken him through a difficult childhood and a sticky patch in early adolescence. They had been both firm and loving. They should have been allowed to adopt him, but the authorities frowned on 'cultural mismatches'. It did not matter, they had adopted each other.

He was amazed at Mark. He wanted to stay on the estate, to work with the deprived people, to help them. For anyone it would have been tough, but for a black man on a mainly 'white trash' estate, it was an act of considerable courage. It was Mark's character that was his shield. He connected with others in a totally natural sincere way. And in so many practical ways he provided help and support. Even the worst thugs treated him with respect.

Therefore the attack by Masters and his group the day before was particularly worrying. Masters was both incredibly ambitious and ruthless and was prepared to suffer the opprobrium of his peers to get his way. Mark had made it clear that he would not tolerate Masters' drug dealing. Masters and his cohorts had got a lot more than they had bargained for, but Douglas felt sure that he would try again.

He looked at his watch. Mark was late, but that was not unusual. It was his Sunday afternoon prayer session and open forum and it often went on until late. Looking up, his eyes caught a figure coming through the broken iron gates of the park and toiling up the hill towards him. It was one of the girls from Mark's group.

"Mark's been shot!" she gasped at him through a tear stained face as she came up to him. He must have been on his way to meet you when it happened.

The next hour was horrendous. Mark was dead. He really should have gone back to his foster parents and helped to console them, but he knew what they would do. There would be intense grief and rage. Followed by prayers for the souls of those who had carried out this act and asking for forgiveness for their own anger. He would see them later, when they would do what he felt was right, which was to remember Mark's life.

He also found out what had happened. He caught Bill Baxter in the stairwell of one of the blocks of flats. It was not an accident. He had waited for Baxter, who was luckily alone. Baxter was one of Masters' thugs, but definitely the weak link. The youth was already pale and his breath stank of vomit, when Douglas grabbed him. He had been terrified of Grant and told the full story after only a hint of a threat of violence.

Bill Baxter, Ed White, Emma Barnes and Johnny Masters had ambushed Mark on his way to meet Douglas. However, despite the odds Mark was still gaining the upper hand. Then Masters had asked Barnes for the gun and shot Mark twice in the stomach. He had laughed and jeered, as Mark had lain dying. Bill said that he himself had been physically sick and Masters had mocked him as well.

Douglas had then informed a policeman at the crime scene what he had been told and gone back to his foster parents to tell them how Mark had died and to join the mourning. He had naively expected the police to quickly apprehend the perpetrators.

By the morning of the second day, it was clear that nothing was being done. Johnny Masters was swaggering about the estate as if he owned it. The police had left the crime scene and were nearly invisible. Only a few local residents who had heard the shots were questioned. None of the obvious suspects were touched, even though under the most gentle of questioning Bill Baxter would have told all.

Johnny Masters was now planning to consummate his authority by bringing a massive amount of cocaine to the estate, as Douglas learned this when he waylaid Baxter again. He also learned that it was a cut-price deal, which a contact of Johnny's was ripping off from a big supplier called Charlie Lomax.

Douglas knew vaguely of Lomax from his father's contacts. He also still knew one of those men, who would pass information for him to Lomax. Here was an opportunity for revenge. An opportunity that he would not miss.

The purchase would take place that night up in the hills above the estate at the site of an abandoned copper mine. Johnny and Emma Barnes would go. Emma was part of the deal, as the contact liked 'a bit of rough'.

Douglas parked his car in a secluded layby well away from the rendezvous spot and walked through the woods to a hill that provided a vantage point overlooking the clearing and overgrown spoil heaps that indicated the presence of the 18th century mine. The shaft itself was still there, surrounded by a broken down, rusty barbed wire fence, towards the back of the clearing.

Douglas had arrived a good hour early, but he had only just hidden himself in a bush and pulled out his binoculars when two cars drove into the clearing from the adjacent road, each containing three men. The vehicles were driven to the far end of the clearing and parked out of sight. The men walked back and hid themselves in bushes near the mine entrance.

The shadows continued to lengthen, but the sun had still not set, when half an hour later a white van drove into the clearing from the road. A burly man got out and lit a cigarette. He was concentrating on the cigarette and did not notice the five men approaching him until they were quite close. Douglas could not hear what was happening, but he did see one of the men hit the burly man with something hard and the man falling. It was at this point that the doubts about what he had done first began to set in.

Two of the other men then kicked the burly man as he lay on the ground and then picked him up while the third man hit him repeatedly in the face. Douglas felt his armpits turning sweaty and a dreadful feeling of nausea. Was this what he wanted?

One of the remaining men climbed into the white van and drove it out of sight at the far end of the clearing. The fifth stood and watched the burly man getting beaten. Douglas focussed on him. He was older than he remembered, but there was no question that was Charlie Lomax.

Suddenly there was a shrill whistle from the man who had remained secluded near the mine entrance. The white van door was slammed shut and the four men disappeared again dragging the burly man with them.

A large Volvo saloon drove into the clearing. Douglas recognised it as one of the 'estate's cars', which were available for anyone to drive. They were originally stolen and then left operational on the estate for general use. Two people got out. One was Johnny Masters and the other Emma Barnes. She was wearing an extremely short skirt, probably for the benefit of the contact. She was also moving erratically. Johnny made a grab for her, but she danced away towards the broken down fence guarding the shaft. She jumped the remnants of the fence and began to dance about on the lip of the shaft making faces at Johnny. She must be high on something thought Douglas.

She then stopped and pointed to the four men who were advancing behind Johnny Masters. He turned and even from half a mile away Douglas sensed him freezing.

"No, no you silly bitch!" thought Douglas, as he watched aghast as Emma Barnes pulled from her hand bag a gun and began to point it in the direction of the advancing men. Silently, something thrust her back and she fell backwards into the shaft. By the time he heard the crack of the pistol her falling body was already out of sight.

"Oh God, no!"

He could see Johnny waving his arms about and then he fell. The crack of the retort came as he hit the ground. His body was pitched into the shaft. The final act was when they dragged the burly man back into the clearing. Something was held to the man's head and it jerked. Douglas did not need the confirmation of the delayed sound of the shot to know what had happened. His body was thrown down the shaft as well. Now, the gloom was deepening rapidly as the sun set.

Gareth Anderson stared, thoughtfully, at the bowed head of Douglas Grant. Gareth's failure had cost Professor Draper his life. The failure of the Manchester police had cost this man his soul.

"Thank you, Dr Grant." he said, gently, "We will get your statement typed up and ask you to sign it."

"Any questions or comments on what we have heard," he asked in a more normal tone, looking at DI Wilkins.

"Only to say," said Wilkins, "That what Dr Grant has said is consistent with what we have found so far, except to say that, of course, Emma Barnes did not die."

"Didn't she?" countered Grant, lifting a trembling hand, his voice breaking, "Haven't you looked into her eyes?"

"But how?" he asked, his voice more normal, as if answering the concerned looks, "How could she have survived? And in such good health? She looks better now than when I last saw her."

The two police officers exchanged a glance, but said nothing.

CHAPTER 19

Ella picked up the tray that had been left by the policewoman and began to tuck into the battered fish, chips and peas. Despite all the disasters, she had not yet lost her appetite. The food had come from the police canteen upstairs in Bridewell police station and was thus freshly prepared. She herself languished in the police cells in the basement. There seemed to be several groups of about four or five cells and she was in a group all by herself. She estimated the time as just after mid-day. She still wore her party dress of the night before, but the police had given her a regulation, sweatshirt to put on. She was glad of it. It was warm and hid her exposed cleavage, which had been making her feel vulnerable.

After finding Draper's body, the previous night had become a nightmare. The police had arrived and had promptly arrested her under her real name - Emma Barnes. How strange that name had sounded in her head as if it belonged to a stranger. A stranger whose memories and guilt she carried.

She had been hustled away in a police car, sitting in the back seat between a young female detective and a middle-aged balding, overweight man with wispy brown hair. The man appeared to be the senior detective present and exhibited a barely concealed distaste for Ella.

The interrogation about Draper's death lasted two hours. The overweight detective had been as nasty as modern procedure would allow. Ella had asked for a solicitor and the duty solicitor had been called in. Ella was under no illusions, duty solicitors worked closely with the police and normally asked their clients to confess and plead guilty, since it would probably result in a reduced sentence. However, she was glad of his presence, since he intervened to object to the worst of the detective's badgering.

The interrogation had concentrated on two damning pieces of evidence: why had she been holding the gun when the others had arrived and, to her

surprise, why had Draper a scrap of paper in his pocket with the two words
- Emma Barnes - on it. She had explained that she had picked up the gun
in a state of shock, after finding the body. This was partially true, she
simply omitted to say that the state of shock was induced by her realisation
that it was her own gun. On the scrap of paper, she, with complete
honesty, but little success, pleaded ignorance.

She was surprised that she had been left in peace that morning. There
had been no visitors. She was totally on her own again. The loneliness was
depressing. Thinking of Kevin resulted in tears streaming down her face.
She had had to concentrate on holding herself together.

The situation was not as bad as when she had been stuck down the
shaft. There was no danger of immediate death. But there was a
hopelessness about it, which she had not felt before. She knew where it
came from. Previously her prison was only the smooth walls of the disused
shaft, now it was the whole panoply of modern, complex human society. It
was like being Kafka's hero in the trial - except that her crime was much
better defined.

She had barely finished her fish and chips and the over strong cup of
cold tea served with it, when the female detective and a policewoman
arrived. They took her upstairs back to the interrogation room. The room
was about twelve by twelve feet and furnished with a simple table and five
straight back chairs. On the table was a small cassette recorder. The walls
were painted with a pale yellow gloss that in places had chipped off
exposing rough plaster underneath. One of the chairs was already occupied
by the same duty solicitor as the night before, who gave her a false smile of
welcome.

She had barely sat down in the seat indicated when the door of the
interrogation room opened again and in walked the portly, hostile detective
of the night before, accompanied by a younger man who was new to her.
The stranger viewed her with almost clinical curiosity. The overweight
detective went through the standard speech, during which Ella learnt that
the younger man was from the Manchester force, and he then indicated to
the policewoman to start the tape recorder.

"Would you like to tell me about the gun?" he barked, as his opener,
"and this time the truth would be helpful."

"I have nothing to add." said Ella, calmly focussing on a chipped piece
of plaster behind the detective's head.

"Well, I have!" he responded, "That gun has the same type of clay on it
as that at the bottom of the old mine workings where we found the bodies.
It is the same calibre as the weapon that killed Mark Ashton on Mantree
estate. Ballistics can establish that it is the same weapon. It is your gun.
Can you deny it?"

Ella was silent. She felt unnerved and trapped.

"I thought not," continued the detective before she had time to recover, "I am therefore charging you, Emma Barnes, with the murder of William Draper and…"

As he intoned automatically the required spiel, Ella stared at him. She felt completely numb. She could not believe that it was happening.

She was then lead back down to her cell and the door locked behind her. The undigested, deep-fried lunch sat like a brick in her stomach. God was she going to puke.

Two floors above acting detective sergeant Michael Wilson groaned. His left leg was hurting again. Nothing so unusual about that except that he no longer had a left leg. It had been amputated above the knee. His own fault, he had stepped in front of a bus. Most of his body had taken a bruising, but his leg had gone under the wheel and had been crushed. This had appeared to end his career in the police.

He lived alone, a confirmed bachelor, with no lover of either sex or need for one, his work had been everything. Enforced inactivity was not to his liking. He had his golf, which got him out, but few other interests - at thirty five he was too young to fill his time in the easy chair watching television or reading. He was a small man, nearly bald with the remnants of his ginger hair cut short. He was still wiry and strove to keep himself fit as best he could.

After four months recuperation, not working had been driving him crazy and he had begged his former employees to take him back. They had finally taken him on a twelve-month contract. This had just been renewed for a further year.

He was part, almost the only part, of Operation Cleansweep. His mission was to review unsolved cases and with the new forensic methods available, particularly DNA testing, to determine, if the case should be reopened. He was able to visit suspects and ask them if they were prepared to furnish a DNA sample and was supplied with a bewildering variety of young DC's as assistants to accompany him on these.

These visits had provided him with his one staggering success. A middle-aged man, whom he had gone to visit, had broken down and confessed to killing a young woman. They had hardly arrived when it happened. The man clearly had a conscience and was haunted by what he had done. The young, previously slightly bored male DC, who had gone with him, had been extremely impressed.

Ironically, the only DNA that had been recovered from the body was that of another suspect who had already admitted to having had sexual intercourse with the victim earlier in the evening.

The man was relieved to have finally confessed. The woman's family were pleased that the perpetrator had been finally caught. So the whole case had left a pleasant feeling of justice having been served.

But of the other ten cases he had looked at - nothing. He sighed. Took a paracetamol for his non-existent leg and picked up another file. Maybe more luck on this one.

CHAPTER 20

"Move house!" Margaret Murdoch glared at her husband angrily, "Dump our poor girls in Bishopston - or worse! You really have no sense, Richard."

Richard stared unhappily at his wife. He knew that this was another argument with his wife that he was going to lose, but he still felt that he had to go through the motions.

"But dear," he continued stubbornly, "We just do not have the money coming in at present to sustain this house and the girls' schooling.

"Richard, you are now the head of department that will mean a pay rise."

"But nowhere near enough," countered Richard, "And the position isn't confirmed yet."

"Nonsense!" responded his wife firmly, "Bill Draper was on the verge of setting up lucrative contracts with industry. Do you know what sort of consultancy fees that they pay these days? If they need someone, and they need you because you have Grant and Hansen."

"Grant hates my guts, he now hates Kevin's guts and Kevin is probably a broken man. The industrial work is very unlikely to go any further."

"Well you have to make sure that it does." shot back Margaret, her eyes glaring, "Go and visit them, bring them on board. Richard you mustn't let the girls down."

Richard stared at her. There was no getting around Margaret when she was like this. There were tears in her eyes and her hands were trembling with emotion.

"OK Margaret." he said, bowing to the inevitable, "I'll see what I can do. I will visit Kevin today. He is always in on a Sunday."

In fact, he thought, Margaret was, as usual, correct. He should visit

Kevin today. He was in a terrible state on Friday after Draper's death and Ella's arrest. He had already made one known suicide attempt and this time Ella was not there to stop him.

"I will take the girls to Sunday school and then to their piano lessons today. That will leave you free to visit Hansen and Grant. Grant is the harder one, so don't put it off. I know you."

Richard felt trapped. Still let's start with the easier one. At least, he should get some sort of civil welcome.

This was a bad weekend and Kevin was dreading Monday. What would people say to him? How could he ever look anyone in the eye again? He had brought a murderer into their quiet academic life. How she had fooled him. He was so soft. He should have told her to leave his house. Instead he had allowed her to seduce him, to wrap him around her little finger, until she had struck again.

It was Sunday lunchtime. So far he had spent the day brooding in his easy chair in his small front room. Yesterday several journalists had called, but today, so far, had been quiet. He had been living on tea, since Friday night. He had been unable to eat. Even now, when he thought of what had happened a clammy feeling would break out and he would feel somewhere between fainting and vomiting. It was getting better, though, but he still didn't feel up to eating anything.

The doorbell rang with such suddenness that it seemed to cut right through him. The last thing he wanted was to meet anyone, journalists or the police. The doorbell rang again.

He cautiously got up from his easy chair and keeping as far as possible from the bay window peered through it. He could see the back of his caller. It looked like Richard Murdoch. He let his breath out. Richard would be sympathetic. With a feeling of intense relief he opened the door.

"Afternoon, Kevin," said Richard with a smile, "Hope that you don't mind, but I thought that I would come round to see how things were going. It must have been a rough day yesterday?"

"God, yes," replied Kevin, feeling tired and a little shaky, "Come on in. Would you like some tea - or coffee?"

"I would love a cup of tea," responded Richard, with a surprising amount of enthusiasm.

Although Richard's presence was lifting his spirits, Kevin still managed to somehow not get the tea made and Richard came and did it for him.

At last they were sitting down with their tea, Kevin in the easy chair and Richard to his right and turned towards him on the short sofa.

"I have heard that Douglas Grant is a complete mess, seeing Ella seemed to completely blow his mind. He, apparently, was ranting on about her being one of the undead bent on revenge. Though why her avenging spirit should be after him is completely unclear," said Richard lightly.

"That stuck up fiancée of his is also behaving a bit oddly. I went into the Department yesterday - just to check if there was anything ultra-urgent - and found her going through Draper's desk. And there was an indication that she had also been through his filing cabinets. God knows what she was after or expected to find. I wasn't aware that they even knew each other outside a couple of brief meetings at our wonderful receptions."

While saying this Richard's tone had been light and conversational, but he now focussed his eyes on Kevin.

"But how's Ella? The poor kid has had a real double whammy. Personally, I find it hard to believe the things that are being said about her. I've always found something quite fine and sensitive within her," said Richard, with feeling.

"Is it true that she is denying shooting Draper? "

"I'm not sure." stammered Kevin.

"Not sure!" repeated Richard, querulously, "She must have said something?"

"Well I haven't seen her since Friday night." answered Kevin, who was now beginning to feel a little uncomfortable.

"Dammed police!" exclaimed Richard, vehemently, "Surely they can't keep you from visiting her?"

Now Kevin was feeling very hot and bothered as embarrassment swept over him. He had not expected anyone to back Ella and certainly not so strongly.

"I'm afraid that I haven't tried." he answered weakly.

"Richard," he continued, feeling a desperate urge to justify himself, "She fooled me - she used me, made me bring her here to escape from her crime - the murder of Grant's brother of all things. And then when she is exposed for what she is she goes and kills the Prof. Maybe he was trying to stop her escaping. And that gun she had. She had it here all the time in this house; she could have killed me. I feel so bad. If it had not been for me being so weak, I would have left her there in that dreadful forest. I would not have even been there. I feel so ashamed. How am I going to face everyone tomorrow? How am I going to face Grant?"

Kevin stopped. He had run out of energy. Now all he could hear was the ticking of his clock. He tried not to look at Murdoch, but was aware of his colleague's eyes upon him. The silence stretched out ten, twenty seconds. Kevin felt the cold sweat starting to break out on his face. He wanted the floor to open up and swallow him. He thought that he could sense the other man's anger - his contempt. He dared to look. Richard was looking at him, as if he was something unpleasant that he had just found on his shoe, but then a light smile flickered briefly over his face.

"You're quite right, of course," began Richard, mildly and surprisingly, "The woman is quite despicable and has done you immense harm, making you unable to face your colleagues. Good God the bitch even saved your life - not to mention your career. The vicious cow even gave you her love."

Richard looked Kevin straight in the eye and added in a much softer voice, "I'm sure it was genuine, Kevin, because if it wasn't I would have seduced her."

Kevin felt in turmoil. What Richard had said had turned the world on its head. Everything that she had done for him had been for the better. Even when she had taken over his car, he had been going nowhere. He would have been stuck the night there, in that dreadful forest. His life - he thought of a life in hospital, in constant agony. A failed paracetamol suicide was hell - a world of pain. She had saved him from that - or death. His work - not only did he have his job, but also he was doing work that he enjoyed, that he was good at. Richard was correct; everything that she had done for him had been for his advantage. And her love, don't forget her love. He remembered the feel and passion of her and what she aroused in him. She was the first woman to need him as a man and he had let her down.

Now she was in prison - alone and abandoned.

"Some lover," he thought bitterly, "No one could rely on him."

"Oh God!" he voiced out loud, "What must she think of me? I'm so ashamed."

He slumped back in the chair and stared miserably at his cup of cold untouched tea.

"And what are you going to do about it," intervened Richard, brutally, "Sit on your arse and feel sorry for yourself, as usual. Or try and put it right."

"I don't know." said Kevin, desperately.

"Well, I do!" continued Richard, relentlessly, "I think that they have taken her to Bridewell. I will give you a lift. It should be easy to park there on a Sunday."

"Richard, what will she say to me? She must really hate me by now."

"Kevin, stop thinking of yourself. If she bawls you out, it's only what you thoroughly deserve. But I'll bet that she doesn't. She's in deep trouble and probably faces years in jail. She'll be glad of all the support that she can get, especially from you."

Richard turned off Gloucester Road at the Zetland Road lights. He liked his Ford Focus. It was a comfortable car to drive. The quiet tones of an Enya CD calmed him. He had left Kevin at Bridewell, with a cup of machine coffee stuck in his hand. Kevin had looked suspiciously relieved that he would not be allowed to see Ella straight away. But Richard had little doubt that he would stay, leaving would require too much initiative.

He felt pleased with himself. He could not help liking Ella and what did he care about Draper and Grant's sanctimonious brother. She would probably welcome Kevin with open arms. A dark thought at the back of his mind came to the fore. What would Margaret say? There was no doubt that if Kevin supported Ella, it would not endear him to Grant. And bringing Grant and Kevin together was one of his key objectives. So what? Margaret need never know that he was responsible.

He drove across the Downs and down the road ultimately leading to Avonmouth, via his own home at Stoke Bishop. But it was here at the top of this road in one of the big houses on the right that his target lay. He stopped opposite the house, got out of his car and crossed the road to where a drive led up to a large two-storey structure. The nest of his enemy, he thought. This was Karen Reading's house and it was here that he had to face Douglas Grant.

He hesitated behind the shelter of a low tree before turning to start up the drive. This was going to be very difficult. It would be hard to hide his dislike of the man. And he was not expecting a particularly civil welcome. It was important to stay calm, not to allow himself to become angry whatever the provocation - or to become sarcastic.

He rang the bell beside the impressive heavy oak front door, which opened slowly to reveal a small, elderly, grey-haired woman in a pink housecoat. He introduced himself and asked if Dr Grant was in. The woman took him into the hall and asked him to wait, while she enquired.

She knew very well whether Grant was in or not, Richard thought to himself. This was a woman, who was used to being circumspect.

He was ushered along the imposing hallway with oak doors leading off it. The woman opened one and led him into a small room. This room was only about 12 feet square and was sparsely furnished with a very fine, oak drinks cabinet. The housekeeper opened a far door and stood back to allow Richard to pass through.

Mentally bracing himself, Richard walked into the room. It was a large expensively furnished room. At the far end, velvet curtains were drawn back from the French windows that led out into a well-maintained garden. On one wall were two beautiful dark-oak glass cabinets both full of a fine collection of ceramic thimbles. In front of these facing towards the fireplace on the opposite wall was a magnificent leather settee. There were also two matching leather armchairs and another settee arranged in an arc. A massive floor mounted television stood proudly on one side of the fireplace and on the other an expensive hi-fi system. In the armchair opposite Richard sat Karen and in the one nearest him with his back to him sat Grant.

Karen turned a pale face towards him – her expression being a mixture of both alarm and apprehension. Douglas Grant rose stiffly from his chair and turned his white, bandaged face towards Richard. Despite himself Richard could not help feeling sorry for the man. He looked worse than ever.

Cordially, but with a tired, sick voice, Grant offered Richard a space on the settee and asked if he would like a cup of tea.

"Yes, that would be lovely." Richard answered, "I've come to see how you are. I gather that you had a particularly rough time on Friday night."

Grant's voice shook and weakened as he answered.

"Seeing that woman was a terrible shock. She is the last person I would have expected to turn up at one of our functions. Kevin is such a weakling. I do not know how he could do it."

"I had met her myself, prior to that evening when I visited Kevin's. I must say as mitigation to Kevin that she was very convincing," responded Richard, choosing his words carefully.

"Is that why you have come?" asked Grant, with some vehemence, "To argue Kevin's case."

"No," lied Richard, smoothly, "You must decide that for yourself. In the light of recent events, I could quite understand if you would find it impossible to work with him."

"It's worked out well for you hasn't it Richard? Draper is dead and you are now the acting head of the department. It is well-known that you two did not get on."

Richard caught the sharpness in the accusing tone and was relieved to be able to delay his answer by accepting the cup of tea that had just been proffered and taking a sip.

"There is no point in pretending I liked the man. I didn't. But I would not have wished him dead. The violence of it was shocking."

"Since I am now your acting boss, I would like to say that I do not expect you to be in next week. I think you need some recovery time. Let me know if there is anything that you need from work and I will bring it to you." Richard flung a glance at Karen as he made the last remark and caught her anxious expression. He had not forgotten her strange visit to Draper's office on Saturday morning.

"No." replied Grant, "There is nothing I need. God! I seem to spend my time off work these days in an emotional mess."

"Don't worry," replied Richard, kindly, "Everyone knows what you have been through."

The door closed silently behind him and Richard walked down the substantial drive to where his car was parked outside.

He felt a warm feeling of satisfaction. He had been sympathetic to Grant and had not lost his temper. In addition, he was now convinced that Karen's visit to Draper's office was completely unknown to Grant. He was sure that his silence on this had put her in his debt. He had done all that Margaret had wanted. Or had he? On reflection, she was sure to find fault with a job that was only half done. No matter, he would just have to put up with her tirade. He was sure that he had done all that was possible.

CHAPTER 21

Kevin stared at the empty plastic cup in his hand. The bottom was still stained with the coffee he had drunk over an hour ago. He felt a desperate desire to leave. Ella would surely denounce his cowardice and lack of loyalty. It had all seemed so clear when Richard had left him here. Now he was not so sure. He eyed the exit. All he had to do was walk out and the nausea and fear would go away. But then tomorrow he would have to face Richard. Indecision glued him to his seat.

Finally, he began to rise. The waiting had gone on long enough. He would tell Richard how he had waited and waited. But Richard would ask why he had not asked the duty sergeant. Kevin looked across to the counter. It was deserted. Now he could go. He walked to the exit, but before he could reach it, the double doors swung open and in walked four large policemen, two abreast. Kevin moved aside to let them in.

"Excuse me, sir!" shouted a voice from behind him. "It's OK to see her now."

Kevin swung round. The sergeant, a short, round-faced balding man, was smiling at him and was lifting the counter flap so that he could pass through.

"Sorry for keeping you waiting. But you know how it is."

With the escape route blocked by the entering policemen, Kevin had no choice, but to move towards the beckoning sergeant and pass behind the counter. His heart was somewhere in his mouth and he felt that his feet were barely touching the ground.

The sergeant led him down a narrow, white-painted corridor to a door at the end, which he opened and stood back to let Kevin through.

In the room was a small table with three seats around it. At one of them sat a policewoman of ample proportions who look liked her uniform had been shrink-wrapped. A fourth chair sat against the wall to his right and was well filled by a burly male policeman, whose bull neck hung over his collar. Both their size and their formal uniforms dominated the room and at first Kevin thought that they were the only people present.

He then saw Ella. She sat at one of the other chairs at the table. Her face was downcast and grey. As it turned to him, Kevin could see that even the penetrating blue eyes were misted and diffuse. Her whole body seemed shrunken, dwarfed and overwhelmed by the others in the room.

The apprehension that Kevin had felt melted away. The vulnerability that had only shown in Ella in tiny chinks before was now fully revealed. Without hesitation, almost without thought, he walked across the room and took her in his arms, as she began to rise from the chair. She flung her arms around his neck and her whole body convulsed with massive sobs. The tears streamed down her face.

"Oh Kevin, I'm so sorry," she sobbed, "I lied to you, told you stories. But I'm so glad you came, I just need you."

She rubbed her tear-wet face against his. Finally, she broke away and they both sat down at the table. For a further long moment she looked at him, her face alight the tears gone.

"I didn't think that you would come," she said, breaking the long silence, "I'm just so glad to see you – so glad."

Kevin noticed that her eyes were clearing, the gaze becoming steady – alive. He felt that, for once that he had done the right thing. Richard had been right, Ella deserved his support.

At last her gaze changed from a wet happiness to a more thoughtful look. "But you must know the truth, Kevin. It is better if I tell you than you hear it from others. You have probably heard some of it already."

Kevin looked into her tear-stained face and their hands met across the table. He was vaguely conscious of the other two people in the room, but their presence now seemed remote. He focussed on Ella. He knew that some of what he would hear he would not like – possibly even make him feel ill. But he also felt strangely elated. He was ready, not just to listen, but to support. He looked into her deep blue eyes.

She was conscious of his dark brown eyes looking at her. His visit had been so unexpected. She had given him up, not expected him to have the strength. The tiny cell had enclosed her, limiting her world to a fold down bed, a washbasin and a metal toilet. Her strength had gone. The spirit that had kept her going in the pit had left her. The bars that complex human society put round you entrap the inner soul far more effectively than any mindless shaft. She had been totally alone.

She had thought that he was too weak. She had imagined him sitting alone in his tiny front room damning her and his own weakness in allowing himself to get involved. Now he was here – where she needed him. But she had to tell him. He had to know everything. She hesitated slightly, as she felt the presence of the two police officers, but they knew nearly everything anyway. She took a deep breath and gripped his hand more tightly. She was still so afraid that he would run.

"I had nothing to do with Draper's death. How he came to be killed with my gun I do not know. That's why I picked the bloody thing up. I was so stunned. After Grant recognised me and was having that fit I fled into the cafeteria. I had just decided to return and face the music when I heard two shots. I went to investigate and found him. That's all I know."

That was the easy bit, she thought; though it was strange how untrue the truth sounded. Kevin was looking at her with apprehension showing in his face. She sensed that her denial was a relief to him. It left him with no hard choices. What came next was going to be harder.

"It all began what seems a very long time ago, but was really only about a year ago when I really started to hang around with Johnny Masters and started being his steady. He was different, very strong and determined to be top dog. I was going nowhere fast. I was already dabbling with drugs and it's amazing how quickly they sap your will. I saw in Johnny a route to wealth and escape. It didn't take him long to introduce me to cocaine. I had no idea what a grip it had on me until I couldn't get it."

"I began losing weight. I was going the same way as my mother, except I wasn't going to last as long."

"I had thought that I was Johnny's girl, but really I was his whore. Once I was of no more use to him he would have dropped me. I can see that now. I didn't want to see it then."

"He hated Mark Ashton, because Ashton stood in his way. He represented an alternative source of power an alternative pole of attraction. Ashton was strong as well and Johnny did not frighten him. There was not room for two of them and Johnny was determined to fix Ashton."

"Of course, what Johnny wanted I wanted. I was so besotted with my visions of what I would be with Johnny in charge on the estate."

"We tried a bit of serious physical violence, we cornered Ashton and a friend who turned out to be Ashton's foster brother, Douglas Grant, and intended to give them a good kicking. It didn't work out like that."

"Both were extremely good at martial arts and it was Johnny and the two others in the gang who got the kicking."

"Afterwards, Johnny was furious. Once the news got out that he had taken a beating then his power on the estate would have been reduced, possibly even ruined. He couldn't let that happen. He had to try again."

Ella stopped for a minute to clear her throat. But she was actually remembering what would be the first omission in her story. Johnny had said to her to be sure to bring the gun, next time and she had. Had she known he was going to use it? It was a question that she could not answer.

"Johnny had somebody in a block of flats with binoculars watching out for Ashton and we were keeping in contact by mobile phone. It was Sunday afternoon and we knew that Ashton would be running his usual open forum at the local community centre. I had been there myself a few times. There was no doubt that he was good. He made religion entertaining and entertainment religious. He knew how to connect, how to make you feel good and optimistic about yourself - and get his message across."

Ella shook her head. How could she have been part of an evil plot to destroy such a man - for what? So that she could be part of the number one criminal gang on the estate? It would not even have happened. Her reward would indeed have been death.

She became aware of Kevin looking at her. Little beads of sweat stood out on his pale forehead and he looked worried and anxious. She could not take too long. He would not last.

"He played into our hands. He was probably heading towards the park and was taking a short cut down a quiet residential side street, with an ideal isolated stretch by an abandoned school."

My former school, thought Ella, shut down by the local authority after coming bottom of the national schools' league tables. The pram pushers' school it was called, because of the number of schoolgirl pregnancies. There had been five in her class alone.

"We drove there in one of the estate's pool cars and waited for him out of sight by the school. There were four of us. The three boys were armed with baseball bats. This time he would get his beating. We were wrong. He was like a Jackie Chan film. I think that they only managed to land one blow on him and that was a glancing blow on his shoulder. He had kicked Johnny hard in his leg leaving him limping and furious. The other two had lost their baseball bats and were set to run, as Ashton turned towards Johnny, Johnny shot him twice in the stomach."

Ella paused. Conscious that she had omitted to say where Johnny had got the gun.

"Ashton fell immediately to his knees and then sank to the ground. It was obvious that he was in great pain. Johnny mocked him, laughed at him asked him where his God was now. I think that Ashton was trying to pray, but within a minute his eyes glazed over and we knew that he was dead."

"Johnny was triumphant, but in a defensive sort of way. He knew that the others were all shocked and horrified. They could also see themselves ending up in jail. Bill Baxter actually puked and Ed White looked shaken."

And how did she feel? Ella reflected to herself on her own feelings. Yes there had been a momentary triumph, but then seeing Ashton lying dying in agony, while Johnny literally danced around him - that was the turning point. It only became clear later, but that was because she had been numbed with cocaine. It was a moment that continued to haunt her."

She felt tears coming to her eyes. She could not stop them and she found herself sobbing. Kevin put his arm around her. She turned her face against his, her tears wetting his cheek.

"It's so hard!" she sobbed, "I can never forget that moment. Poor Mark Ashton, he didn't deserve to die like that."

Kevin was looking at her. His face was extremely pale and his breathing had become shallower. His hand was very sweaty, but it gripped hers firmly. He was going to stay, though he might pass out.

As her sobbing receded, Ella took a deep breath.

"There is more, I'm afraid. Strangely, the next day we were still free. The police had not even tried to question us. Johnny was really swaggering. He had got rid of the most potent force on the estate opposed to him and had done so without retribution, without even being made to feel uncomfortable. Now everybody on the estate knew who was in charge."

"He decided that now was the time to bring in a new load of cocaine. He had a contact, who could get the stuff cut price. I didn't know it then, but it was actually being knocked off from a big dealer called Charlie Lomax. I think that Johnny must have been in self-destruct mode by then. You would have thought that after the murder, the most natural thing to have done would have been to have gone to earth – not Johnny!"

"A rendezvous was set up the following evening at an old copper mine in the hills above the estate. Only Johnny and I would go." Ella hesitated, "Johnny had persuaded me to give the contact a good time. It would 'lubricate the transaction' he had said. It just shows how far I was sinking."

"We drove up in one of the pool cars. I was clearly not happy, so Johnny had persuaded me to take more cocaine. As it turned out I had taken far too much."

"We arrived at the mine and it appeared that the contact was not there yet. I am a bit hazy about what happened next. After getting out the car, I took it in my head to cross the broken down fence next to the shaft and dance about on the lip. Johnny was really alarmed, which I thought was really fun. I think now he was more concerned about the money I was carrying for the deal than about me."

"It was then that I saw the four men advancing behind Johnny. I could see that three of them were carrying guns. I shouted to Johnny. It was so funny to see the look on his face. I was so high that I thought that I could readily deal with them and I pulled the gun from my bag and started waving it in their direction. It was then that something hit me very hard in my right hand. It was a bullet that I found out later had smashed into the handle of the gun. That handle saved my life, but the force of the blow knocked me backwards. I felt like I was floating down the shaft until I hit the remnants of a large bush at the bottom. I remember vaguely the branches smashing against me."

"I don't think that I was unconscious very long, but for ages, probably about two days I spent most of my time desperately searching for more cocaine. I was at the bottom of a dark pit with sheer walls and two dead bodies and all I could think of was getting more cocaine. The power of the damned stuff is so strong. I licked a wet wall for water, but did nothing else to keep body and soul together.

"Slowly the craving ebbed and as it did I began to realise just how difficult my situation was. I was in a hole about thirty feet deep. The walls had no handholds and appeared unscaleable. The sky was a small grey circle far over my head all around me was a deep gloom. I was both hungry and freezing cold. I had been aware of my two dead companions from the beginning, but at first I hardly cared. Their bodies only represented a promising possible source of cocaine, but there was none on them."

"I had discovered the side passage in my frenzied searching for dope. It was only about 10 yards long and at the end was a deep shaft presumably going to lower levels of the mine. I had almost plunged down it and it still amazes me that I didn't, as it was pitch black. I realised that I had to get warm. Fortunately, I had some matches in my handbag, but had run out of cigarettes. There was a lot of dried wood down there and I managed to get a fire lit. The smoke went straight up and out the roof. A burning ember showed me that there was air rising from the lower shaft. There must have been another entrance somewhere. But there was no way that I could descend the lower shaft and try and find it."

"Both Johnny and the contact, who I knew as Paul Tulley had been shot in the head. Their upper clothes were covered in their blood and probably bits of skull and brain. But I stripped off Tulley's big heavy jacket and put it on and stripped of the trousers from both of them. I put Johnny's on first and then Tulley's much larger pair on top. He had been a bit overweight."

Ella took a sip of water from the plastic tumbler in front of her. She could hear the deep breathing of the policewoman next to her, but it was Kevin's face she looked into. His hand was still on hers, only a little sweaty now, he seemed to be bearing up well and to have recovered from his physical reaction to the description of Mark's death. His body was leaning towards hers, his face showing concern. She hadn't expected him to be so supportive. She hadn't even expected him to be there. He was what she had so badly needed. But how would he cope with the next part.

"It was strange, terrifying and surreal, to be there, the flickering orange glow of the fire causing the dead faces of my companions to appear and disappear. They were both in sitting positions around the fire, as if we were all camping together, except that only one of us was alive.

"Below the wet wall I had found a small pool of water, so there was plenty to drink. But there was no food."

"The one real job I had ever had was working in a butcher's shop for six months. That's why I was getting on at Ashbury's so well, as I was familiar with all the different cuts. I knew how to butcher meat and what to avoid. I also had somewhat vaguer ideas about smoking and drying meat to preserve it. Butchering humans is technically not that different from pigs. Even for me, though, there was an ethical chasm to cross. But what choice did I have?"

Ella stopped. Kevin's hand had become very sweaty again and the rhythm of his breathing had changed. She was also conscious of some restlessness from the policewoman on the other side of her, but she did not turn away from Kevin.

"You had no choice." answered Kevin, hoarsely. His face was now very pale. He was speaking more to give himself a break from Ella's narrative than because he had to. She felt that he was still with her, but was struggling with his imaginings and his physical reaction to them.

Ella turned away from Kevin and faced the policewoman, a pale, round face looked back at her.

"I'm afraid I need the toilet." she said. She didn't, but she felt it would give Kevin time to absorb what she had said and recover.

"I need it too," said Kevin gratefully.

The two police took Ella back towards the cells through the other door, after giving Kevin directions to the public toilet out the door he had come in.

Although going to the toilet had seemed to have taken an age to Ella, she still had to wait a further ten minutes before the other door of the interview room was unlocked and a still pale Kevin was ushered in by a sergeant who then withdrew. There was a hint of vomit on his breath, but his breathing was more regular and he even managed to give her a weak, but encouraging smile.

Ella had decided to skip the details of what she had done next.

How she had stripped the flesh from Tulley's legs, arms and buttocks and hung them over the fire to dry. How she had removed his liver and placed it on the fire on a wide, thin platter she had made from the clay taken from the shaft floor. The human liver is a remarkably large organ. It had lasted her for three days.

She had stripped out some of the subcutaneous fat from the torso and melted it in a large bowl she had made from the wet clay. It had cracked leaking fat into the fire, where it popped and exploded in little balls of flame. She had used it for cooking and for fuelling two little clay lamps that she had made. She even ate some of it alone, hoping that it would help keep her warm and alleviate the effects of a pure meat diet. She had read somewhere that high protein diets put a strain on the kidneys. And that made her think of Tulley's kidneys and his heart. She had recovered both of those. The kidneys she had eaten with the liver, the heart she had cooked and smoked over the fire and eaten later.

There was more. She had found looking at Tulley's lungs fascinating. The man had smoked and it showed. There was both damage and clear evidence of what looked like a tumour. She remembered from a previous encounter how he had wheezed as he had lain on top of her coming to his unloving, animal climax. She hadn't told Kevin about that either.

She had gutted him to stop the body from being contaminated. Two days after death was a long time and the stomach and intestines had already started to swell up, so she had cut them out and buried them in what was her toilet corner of the shaft, well away from the water. His face seemed to wear a disapproving look, so she had hacked off his head and buried it near the guts. The fear of brain disease she had kidded herself with, but it was really that frozen expression.

Now there was only the hollow chest cavity looking at her in the flickering lights, the ribs glistening white. Johnny though was still intact. For the next four weeks he would watch her, as his eyes went black, his body began to swell and the maggots moved in. She would talk to him, shout at him, rage at him, and accuse him of ruining her life of exploiting her. But she knew that it had been destroyed long before she had met him.

She had tried. Between the ages of eleven and fifteen she had almost made it. But then the hormones, combined with cannabis, kicked in and thrust her back where she had come from. She had been in decline ever since and after meeting Johnny had gone into free-fall.

"After dealing with the meat problem and taking care to preserve it, I began sorting out my living area." was all she said, "I found that a fire was a voracious consumer of wood and that to conserve stocks, I had to let it burn at a low level. There were some thick pieces, but even each of these would be consumed in a few hours. By the end, I was almost nearly out."

"Before that just a day or two after sorting myself out, I took ill. I think that I had given myself a chill, when I hadn't taken care of myself, while searching for cocaine."

"I was very bad for a day and must have had a high temperature. I hallucinated. Sometimes Johnny would open his mouth as if to speak to me, sometimes the empty hulk of Tulley would stand up and seem to move towards me. But mainly it was Mark Ashton that I saw. He would be standing there, as he had been dressed on that last day, a huge stain of blood on his shirt. Sometimes he would denounce me as a sinner, sometimes he would be calling on God to forgive me. Always I would shout out that I was sorry, so sorry."

"Over the remaining two and a bit weeks he would come into my dreams, but not when I was awake. Except sometimes, from the corner of my eye, I would think that I had seen him, but as I turned he was gone. But when I slept, he would be there, to denounce or forgive and sometimes just to look."

"In that time, thoughts of my own death only frightened me in the sense that I felt that I had only just started my life that I had rediscovered something that I had lost and that it could be taken away from me. I was determined to survive and to escape. I knew that the chances of anyone finding me were getting less and less as the year wore on. In the summer, there could have been kids and lovers on the ground above, but not in the winter. I would listen for any sounds. Only once did I hear a car and I threw some water on the fire to create a cloud of steam and even tried to shout, but no one came."

"I also tried cutting grooves into the side of the wall to give handholds. At first, I didn't use the knife that I had; it was too valuable to risk. But towards the end as the food began to run out and the shaft began to flood I resorted to it in desperation. I did manage to climb about six feet, but the higher one got the more precarious and slower the work became."

"I was able to supplement my food with some rats that I trapped in a flooded pit that I had dug. I think that they had become trapped there like me, after being attracted by the smell of my food. There were also a few snails."

"I was already starting to feel desperate when the rain came. There had been rain before some showers, which I could easily shelter from, but this was heavy, incessant and went on for days. The tiny amount that had been coming down the wet wall was transformed into a vigorous stream. I was able to channel this into the side tunnel, which gradually sloped down to the lower shaft."

"Then came what seemed to be total disaster, but turned into my saviour. The lower shaft filled completely with water and began to flood the side tunnel. I was in a panic; it was rising rapidly at a rate of two or three feet a minute. Water had to be pouring into the workings somewhere else and rising back up through the lower shaft. I now knew how my rat victims must have felt."

"Very soon it had extinguished my fire and was lapping around my knees. It was freezing cold and the two pairs of trousers I had on began to drag me down. I had to strip off putting on only the light nylon coat that I had worn as it didn't soak up the water and gave some limited protection. I desperately tried making more handholds, this time with a stone hammering on the precious knife, but it quickly broke."

"The water was above my waist and freezing cold, I knew that shortly I would drown or die of hypothermia, whichever got me first. Drowning probably as the water was still rising rapidly. My two lamps were stuck to the wall with damp clay and were still burning, in there light I could see that the two halves of a substantial log that I had burned in half were bobbing about, I pulled them together and lashed them together with Johnny's trousers. I then climbed on to them lying prone along their length."

"The rising waters then reached first one lamp and then the other and I was left in near total darkness. I was freezing, but being now mainly out of the water the heat loss from my body had declined. I twisted around to look upwards and could just make out the not quite so dark circle of the shaft opening."

Ella hesitated in her narrative and looked at Kevin. His face was intent, absorbed, his hand in hers felt dry.

"I thought that I was going to die. I was floating in a half-filled shaft, freezing cold and absolutely no way of getting out. But then I was lucky. The water level in the shaft continued rising and lifted me up to within a few feet of the top, from where there were enough handholds to scramble out. I stood there on the top in the wind and rain not believing my good fortune. I then ran to the shelter of nearby woods."

"I was shivering uncontrollably and desperately needed to warm up. Fortunately, I found a reasonably dry, old foxhole, which I was able to curl up in and let my own body heat do its work. I thought of staying there for the night, but then I saw a car's lights through the trees. I thought of course that it would carry on, but instead it stopped. So I took my chances and I'm so glad I did, because that's how I met you."

"My God!" exclaimed Kevin, "How long were you down the shaft?"

"Oh, I would think about a month." replied Ella.

"And that story about the attempted rape...?" asked Kevin.

"Was just a story, I'm sorry to say" replied Ella.

"You recovered amazingly well. And that night, you drove my car all the way back to Bristol." he said, staring at her with blatant admiration.

She gripped his hand tighter.

"Thanks for always backing me, Kevin." she replied, "Especially now - I feel so much more ready to face the future."

CHAPTER 22

Margaret Murdoch could feel her irritation rising. Richard seemed to think that the day had gone well and that he could now relax. He seemed to have no idea just how much urgent work needed to be done or just how precarious their position was.

"So Kevin should be back at work tomorrow?" she asked.

"Yes, indeed," answered Richard.

"What about his attitude to the Barnes woman?"

"He was going to see her, as I left."

"What! That's bad news. If Grant finds out he is still supporting her he will never work with him. Didn't you try and talk him out of it?"

She scanned Richard's face as she asked that question. She felt her anger rising. He was looking guilty and evasive. The silly fool had done the opposite.

"That was your doing wasn't it? Oh Richard! Think of the girls! If we can't raise more money, they will have to leave Blue Maids School. Do you really want them to go to a Bristol state school? I know you think I make too much of it, but Bristol schools are the worst in the country. I know! I went to one!"

She had almost shouted the last statement and felt herself beginning to shake. The memories came flooding back - horrible memories. How different it would all have been, if she had not gone there.

She took a firm control of herself.

"Ah well, you have done it now. We must look ahead. Tomorrow, you will have to start phoning the professor's industrial contacts. Reassure them as quickly as possible that the work will carry on and please try and give them the impression that you are in control. I'm sorry to be telling you how to do your job, but if you can get some personal commitment from them then that will help you maintain your position, when the senate considers it.

Remember you are just the acting head of department at present."

"I suppose you are right." replied Richard, with a noticeable lack of enthusiasm, "But it does seem rather callous, Draper is barely cold."

"Oh Richard!" exclaimed Margaret, "That's your excuse to ring round. To let them all know that Draper has been killed by a maniac and how terrible it all is. You do have to be diplomatic. And do focus; remember what your real interests are. No more slip-ups like Hansen and Barnes."

Margaret felt herself starting to sag. Trying to get Richard to move was like wading through treacle – hard work and exhausting. She wondered for the umpteenth time why she had married him. The answer was always the same: because the really desirable, well-connected male students could see through her. See into the sadness and distress that lay below the surface. Richard had been the best compromise; apparently capable and ambitious, but without the perception to see beyond her physical attractions.

"Oh! A good school for the girls was so important!" she almost shouted aloud, as her thought processes led her inevitably back to the paramount objective. It was unbearable to think of them being ruined like she had been and the tears began to rise in her eyes.

"What about Doug Grant? Will he be in tomorrow?"

"Not tomorrow," responded Richard, with visible nervousness, "But I think he will be back by the end of the week. I also think that I have Karen Reading on our side. When I was in the department on Saturday morning, I found her going through Draper's, now my, desk. She claimed to be after something for Grant, but I had the distinct impression when I met them today that he knew nothing about it and that she was extremely worried that I would say something. I think that's one she owes me and that she will encourage Grant to return."

"Possibly, but I know you Richard. You think that you are very clever getting something on someone and then you just don't use it. Please be prepared to get heavy. You will need all the leverage that you can get for Grant to work with Hansen, especially after your performance today."

"Yes, you are quite right." responded Richard, with a yawn, "It's only half past nine, but I feel dead beat, if you don't mind, I'm off to bed."

Richard gave her the briefest of pecks on her cheek and went up to bed. They slept in different rooms, so Margaret wouldn't disturb him. She slept for only about four hours at night and – anyway – there was no physical relationship left now.

She watched Richard go. She felt sorry for him. If her life had not gone badly wrong she would not have married him and he would almost certainly have had a plainer, but more understanding, wife. "After all," she thought wryly, "He does seem to like plain women."

Margaret had been standing up, due to her agitation, but now she sat down in her armchair. She gazed round their sitting room with barely seeing eyes.

It was quite large with plain embossed wallpaper and a high, white ceiling. The door to the hall was natural oak. Opposite, a fake coal fire with its dancing gas flames occupied the pale brown tiled fireplace. On the wooden mantelpiece sat a two-year clock, its circular pendulum lazily turning one way and then reversing and turning the other.

A second door, of matching oak, led off the wall to the right of the hall door into the kitchen diner. The kitchen faced southeast and caught the morning sun. It was bright and airy and Margaret loved sitting at the table eating her breakfast and listening to the excited chatter of her two young daughters. Much had gone wrong with her life, but when she thought of them her spirits lifted.

"Without Richard," she thought, "There would have been no girls. Without even that horrendous year at that school, there would have been no girls. They made it all worthwhile, kept her going, made her positive."

"Which is why I mustn't stop." she said aloud to herself, "There is now an opportunity to keep them at Blue Maids, but it is so fragile a thing."

She gave a sigh and picked up the phone. "There is still so much to do."

Richard was soon in bed. He did feel tired. The euphoria of Saturday morning had gone. He felt so foolish. It had taken Margaret no time at all to find out that he had encouraged Kevin to see Ella. The new job would be hard and he had grave doubts that he could keep it. He felt very conscious that he was no Draper. The best thing to do was to act the part, as if it were a role in a play. That thought cheered him up.

Margaret was so single-minded. There were good state schools outside Bristol, but she would not leave Stoke Bishop. Even the schools in Stoke Bishop were not so bad. After all he had gone to a state school, but that was something that he had learned not to remind Margaret of. "You had it easy," she would declare with powerful passion and precious little justification. But there is no way of arguing with passion.

His mind turned to Aggie. She was getting better and would soon be back home. He thought of the visit he had made to the hospital that day. She was cheerful and looking forward to the future. She had been able to embrace him without wincing. He thought of her long black hair with streaks of grey and her big dark brown eyes. She was warm, she was intelligent, but most of all she had feeling, an empathy that made him feel warm and invigorated by her company. She had one daughter by a brief relationship, a happy girl living in London.

He thought again that he would have to confront Margaret, but he knew he would put it off. She would lambaste him over the girls, using them to make him feel a terrible guilt and it would work. His mind began to wander as he slipped into a troubled sleep.

CHAPTER 23

Gareth looked up at the two uniforms standing in front of his desk. Both were well filled one by the ample proportions of WPC Mary Fawcett and the other by the stout figure of PC Jack Davies. They had reported on the meeting of Ella with her boyfriend. The disappointment was that from his point of view nothing had come of it. She had said little that was new and what had been new, was only useful to DI Wilkins. On the Draper case, she was denying any involvement. Monday was not getting off to a good start.

He dismissed the two uniformed officers with a short compliment and turned to face DC Jane Kent, who had been standing against the wall listening to the report.

"There has to be a way of breaking her down on this. I had thought that authorising that meeting with her lover might get somewhere, but nothing."

"I have a thought, sir." said Jane, visibly taking a breath, "I've never been convinced of the racist nature of the attack on the Silverman woman or the attempted attack on Barnes. There were too many other more obvious targets in the neighbourhood. There's even a leading, prominent Zionist in the same street as Silverman. I think that there is a connection between the two that has nothing to do with race. The apparent racism was just a smokescreen to hide it. It is even possible that the Barnes attack was faked. With your permission, I would like to go and have another chat with the immediate neighbours."

Gareth looked thoughtfully at the youthful, DC - her pale complexion, her youth, and her tidy blond hair, cut just above the shoulder. When he had first met her, he had unkindly thought of her as a bimbo; an opinion that he very quickly found himself reassessing. It was the eyes that gave her away, these were large, blue, observant and intelligent. He felt that she would be better employed building the case against Barnes by getting fuller statements from witnesses on the events of that night, but he already had two DC's doing that. He was also very conscious of the lack of motive. Maybe the further enquiries she proposed could throw some light on that. "Mmm, sounds a little tenuous, but might help with motive. OK! But don't spend too much time on it. I'll expect you back by lunchtime."

Jane parked her car outside Kevin's house. At ten o'clock on a Monday morning, there were plenty of empty spaces. She was suspicious that Barnes had staged the attack on herself. It made sense, as she was the known criminal in the case, but why attack Silverman. She didn't go to Kevin's door, but instead knocked on the door of the neighbour. Jane had decided that Rosemary Brown could be the most useful; after all she was also a friend of Rachael Silverman.

She went up and knocked on the blue painted door. The paint was fresh and still smelled of gloss. Rosemary opened the door cautiously. She was shorter than Jane, her grey hair hanging untidily. Jane introduced herself and began to get her identification out of her jacket pocket. Rosemary almost pounced on her.

"Police! Oh please come in! Come in! I am so glad you came. I was thinking of ringing you."

Jane was literally dragged in, and them Rosemary thrust into her face that day's edition of the 'Western Daily Press'.

"There, there on page 2, that man, that was him!" shouted Rosemary pointing to a picture of a thin-faced man half way down the page. "That's the man, I saw outside Rachel's house. He tried to hide his face with a scarf when I looked at him. And I saw him again, watching my house or Kevin's less than a week before someone tried to attack Ella."

Jane stared at the picture. She did recognise the man. His name was Bill Harrison and he described himself as a private enquiry agent. His speciality was debt collection and he had some very nasty enforcers to help him. She also knew vaguely what had happened to him. She had overheard two male DCs sniggering about it in the canteen. Apparently, the man had died from what looked like an autoerotic experiment that had gone wrong, resulting in him strangling himself. Good riddance she had thought to herself at the time.

As she reflected on it, she felt a rising feeling of excitement. This man had violent and unpleasant minions at his disposal. He was not a racist; he would have anyone beaten up if there was money in it.

"Are you sure?" she queried, trying to remain calm and not jump too far ahead without some verification.

"Absolutely!" responded Rosemary, "That big nose and thin face are really quite distinctive and I am usually quite good with faces, anyway."

"How often did you see him?"

"As I said to your colleagues, at least three times. Once just a few doors from Rachel's house and then, let me see – twice outside mine."

"Right outside?"

"No! He was across the street standing at the junction with Acacia Street." As she said this she moved to the window and pointed across the street to a junction about twenty yards to the right."

"It's a reasonable distance." commented Jane.

"My eyesight is still very good for a distance, though I do need reading glasses now."

Jane paused for a moment to read the article under the picture. It just described Morrison as a "well-known private detective" and merely said that his death appeared to be "a tragic accident." No indication there of the man's vicious reputation or the seedy nature of his death. The only hint of something deeper was the appearance of the article, at all. As it stood, it didn't seem particularly newsworthy. The journalist had clearly known more, but had not wanted to go into print at this stage.

"Have you ever heard of this man, before?"

"No, never!"

"May, I borrow this paper? I think I may need it."

"Yes, of course, please keep it. But why would a private detective be interested in Rachael or me – or Ella?"

A good question thought Jane, but not so much a private detective more a gangster. Her mind was racing. If Rosemary was right – and it was a big if – then there was now one at most two clear suspects for the brutal attack on Rachael Silverman. This man's enforcers were known to the police.

Jane struggled to return the discussion back to her original reason for coming.

"Apart from this man do you know of any other possible connection between Rachael Silverman and the woman known to you as Ella Slater?

Rosemary shook her head, doubtfully and then giggled.

"Yes, of course, there is me!"

Jane looked thoughtful for a moment. It was true, but there was probably nothing in it. It looked as though her original line of enquiry was going dry. Still she had managed a rather nice and juicy consolation prize.

"Think carefully, no matter how slight or tenuous, anything at all."

"There is something odd." said Rosemary with a thoughtful frown, "Ella sometimes had a gentleman visitor in the afternoons, a very smart and good-looking man, probably in early middle age. I had seen him there before, when it was just Kevin – I mean Dr Hansen - usually on a Sunday morning. Well the funny thing is I am sure I have seen the same man at Southmead hospital when I have been visiting Rachel. Once he was walking away from her ward and the second time he was actually in Rachel's ward and I had the distinct impression that he had been moving away from Rachel's bed. He was leaving as I came in. That was only a couple of days ago and Rachel is much better and will be coming home shortly. Anyway she looked distinctly flushed, when I came up to her and I wondered if that was her boyfriend."

"She has a boyfriend?"

"Oh yes! She did tell me, but she was very coy about it. I suspected that it was a married man. Poor Rachel, she was married once, but the husband turned out to be a real pig."

The most difficult thing Jane found was to control the rising excitement in her. It should be quite easy to identify Barnes' mysterious visitor, Hansen would tell them even if Barnes didn't.

"Would you be able to identify this man again?"

"Of course, no doubt at all."

Gareth Anderson had to struggle not to lick his lips. He now knew how a tiger felt with a cornered prey. This whole case was frustrating him, but now he had someone, who had been holding something back and were they going to be in trouble. Following a telephone call from Jane on her meeting with Rosemary Brown, he had immediately taken Barnes up for very brief further questioning and the woman had readily admitted, who her mysterious visitor had been, seemingly bemused that the question should be asked.

Dr Richard Murdoch was sitting in his office – his new office. It was a nice big office, reflecting nice big authority and a nice big salary and its previous occupant had been foully murdered. There was no problem of a motive here. He sat in his comfortable chair at his well-polished oak desk, facing down the long table pushed up to it. His face wore a look of officious helpfulness, but underneath there were clear signs of apprehension.

Jane and Gareth sat on opposite sides of the table.

"Sorry to interrupt your lunch," began Gareth, with a glance at the half-eaten sandwich on a plate in front of Murdoch, "But with a murder enquiry, as you will understand, we must follow up leads as quickly as possible."

"No problem, always ready to give whatever help I can."

"Good. We would like to know what your relationship is or was with Rachel Silverman?"

"Rachel! What on earth has she got to do with it?"

"We have reason to believe that there may be a connection with our current enquiry. Now please answer the question."

"We are friends, good friends."

"In fact, you are lovers."

"I think that is a rather impertinent suggestion."

"But it is true. Please don't waste my time, we already have someone on their way to question Miss Silverman."

"You bastards! She is still not well!"

"Then tell us what we need to know and she won't be troubled."

Murdoch looked flushed and upset.

"OK! Yes, we are lovers."

"And what please is your relationship with Emma Barnes –alias Ella Slater? Is she also your lover?"

"I really don't like your tone. I am perfectly within my rights to terminate this interview."

"You are perfectly correct and this interview would have to be continued with a solicitor present to represent you. In that case, of course, we would have to take you down to the station, where you would have to wait until your solicitor arrived. But please let me remind you again that this is a murder investigation. Your co-operation would be very much appreciated."

Murdoch hesitated for a moment considering this option. Gareth watched him. Perhaps he had pushed him too far. Still getting him to the station, leaving him to stew in an interview room, there were advantages to that.

"Very well, I have nothing to hide, Ella and I were good friends and definitely nothing more."

"You find Miss Barnes an attractive woman?"

"Attractive is not quite the word. She is very unusual."

"Whereas Miss Silverman is very ordinary?"

"What are you implying?"

"Was Miss Silverman becoming boring? Perhaps threatening to tell your wife? Maybe becoming too possessive? In short, did she have to be dealt with?"

"What? Are you suggesting that I had anything to do with that attack on her? It's absurd. I am deeply in love with Rachel. To suggest that I could be behind that vicious attack is really going too far!"

Murdoch had become very agitated and his face went through an amazing colour change as the anger swept through his body. A whiteness travelled from the top of his face downwards and then was immediately replaced by a florid redness travelling upwards."

Gareth felt glad of the desk and the table between them.

"I am sorry to have upset you sir," he oozed, apologetically, "But we do have to consider all options, no matter how unlikely."

"You think there is a connection between what happened to Rachel and Draper's death?" asked Murdoch, thickly, as he clearly struggled to quell his temper.

"There is a connection and, I am afraid that connection is you."

Gareth looked ostentatiously around the large office before continuing.

"I have reviewed your evidence concerning the night of Draper's murder and I am afraid to say that I don't find it entirely satisfactory. It implies that while one of your work colleagues was having a fit, you calmly left the room to go to the toilet. Two other gentlemen were in the toilet, when Grant had his 'turn' and neither reported you coming in. So please could you tell us what you actually did?"

Murdoch stared back; his anger of a moment ago had gone. He now had the look of a confused animal at bay.

"When Ella left the room, I followed her. I presumed that she was going to do a runner. Everyone else was still gawking at the exhibition Grant was making of himself. I saw her disappear through the door of the cafeteria across the landing and went in myself. I couldn't see her anymore, but I saw the light coming up the stairs, which led down to the gymnasium. I immediately assumed that she had gone that way and rushed down."

"Did you actually see her go down?" interrupted Gareth.

"No, I can't say that I did. It seemed to be the logical place for her to go. Anyway I could neither see her nor hear her when I got to the bottom of the stairs. The corridor, leading past the changing rooms and back to reception, was dimly lit. It is quite a long corridor and I thought that I would have seen her. So I turned the other way into the gymnasium and left by the fire exit on the opposite side, as I had assumed that that was where she had gone."

"Did you close this door behind you?"

"Yes, I remember, distinctly thinking that I must shut it and doing so. Outside in the dark, I realised that I had completely lost her and was on my way back round to reception, when I heard what turned out to be the two shots."

"Thank you, sir. Now why didn't you tell us this before?"

"I was afraid that I would incriminate Ella."

"It certainly does, but it also places you at the scene of the crime, a man, who by all accounts had an adequate motive, and who has gained significantly from the professor's death."

"I suppose you are correct." answered Murdoch, vaguely, as if some erudite mathematical fact had been pointed out to him.

"To be blunt, Dr Murdoch, you have hindered the police investigation into a very serious crime. You could well be charged. I would also be pleased if you could inform us, if at any time you intend to be away from Bristol."

Gareth got up to leave and Jane Kent followed. The last he saw of Murdoch, as the door closed was his pale face looking anxiously after them. They did not speak to each other until they were in the car.

"At last!" exclaimed Gareth, as Jane started the car, "I feel like we are starting to get somewhere."

"You think that he could have done it?" asked Jane in surprise.

"No, but I think that he could have put Barnes up to it and then went after her to stop her when she was exposed. After all, if he offered Barnes a significant sum of money to do the deed, I bet she would have done it, but he would have not wanted it to go ahead after she had been exposed."

"But how did she manage to get Draper down into the men's changing room?"

"Sex!" exclaimed Gareth, with a laugh, "From what we are learning about the good Professor he had a very roving eye. Which reminds me, someone else with a motive is Mrs Draper, but she has had no known contact with the Barnes woman. Still I think that tomorrow we should pay her a visit and learn a bit more about the Professor. This afternoon, though, there is another suspect to question. I shall stay on to do that myself."

CHAPTER 24

The man entered her cell and the door locked behind him. He was a portly, figure, even shorter than she was, with a red, round face, a short beard joining with his sideboards and small round wire glasses. Behind the glasses small eyes, almost eagerly appraised her.

That morning, she had decided to take the plunge and organise a decent solicitor for herself. Her morale was so much better, since Kevin's visit the day before. She had contacted a legal aid centre and they had said that they would try and get someone. Now, here he was.

"Good afternoon, Miss Barnes," he said in a soft Scottish accent. "My name is Ian McDonald, but please just call me Ian."

"I am a solicitor with the practice of Harper and McDonald, specialising in criminal law. The centre contacted me about your case and I would consider taking it on, if we both mutually agree. However, whatever we decide, you have my complete assurance that anything said here will remain strictly confidential."

Ella looked at him. He was particularly unprepossessing in appearance with a slightly shabby suit, but there was an encouraging vigour about him.

With a short nod of acknowledgement they both sat down.

"So far," began the solicitor, "I have only had a short chat with old George – you know – the duty solicitor. He clearly did not feel it appropriate, at this stage, to say too much, until I was officially representing you, but he did outline the police case. So I would be pleased if you could tell me about the two incidents and how you view them."

Ella took a deep breath and tried to summarise what had happened with Mark Ashton. Her summary of Professor Draper's murder was much briefer.

"So you emphatically deny shooting Professor Draper."

"I do, absolutely."

"But it was your gun that was used?"

"Yes, but I have no idea how it got there."

"How do you explain that the gun is covered in your fingerprints?"

"When I saw it, I picked it up and turned it over in my hands. I just couldn't believe that it was mine."

"You were not wearing gloves then?"

"No, of course not. I wasn't expecting to be handling a murder weapon."

"Have you, yourself, ever fired that gun? Could you fire that gun?"

"Yes, Johnny, the two others and I practised with it, about two months ago. We went into a local wood and shot at tin cans."

"Were you any good?"

"I'm afraid so. None of the rest could ever hit the cans, but I hit them several times."

The solicitor's small eyeballs rolled up in their sockets towards his forehead and almost disappeared and hung there quivering for a few seconds. Whether in disbelief or thought, Ella could not tell.

"Have you ever fired the gun – or any gun - since?" He finally asked.

Ella hesitated trying to remember.

"I was a little out of my head at the mine shaft, but no I am quite sure that I didn't."

"Well, that is the murder charge, but there is also the charge of aiding and abetting murder. You know that it carries the same serious penalties as murder?"

"Yes, the duty solicitor told me," responded Ella, feeling very downcast. She hesitated for a few moments.

"This is strictly confidential, isn't it? Even if I say something that could be seen as incriminating."

"Absolutely!" exclaimed the lawyer. "If I am to represent you it is important that I know all the facts from you, rather than be surprised by them later."

Ella took a deep breath, "I was carrying the gun for Johnny and passed it to him, before he shot Mark Ashton."

"Did the other two present see this?"

"Yes, and it is bound to be in their evidence - with suitable claims of horror and surprise."

"Have the police asked you about this yet?"

"Yes, and I said that it was only when we were going to get the cocaine at the mineshaft, when Johnny gave me the gun. I hadn't had it before then."

The eyes nearly vanished again and went through their little dance, before descending to a more normal position.

"Have you ever, in similar circumstances passed a gun to the late Mr Masters?"

"Yes, it had happened twice before; once with someone trying to muscle in on our patch and once with a social worker. She was trying to stop a client getting drugs," answered Ella, feeling appalled at her former self.

"The social worker, did she complain to the police?"

"Oh yes! But we all just denied it. It was her word against ours."

"So the police were definitely involved in that incident?"

"Yes, very much so."

"In any of the incidents, did you expect Masters to actually use the gun?"

"I don't honestly know. I was both afraid and excited."

"But by the time of the actual shooting he had already threatened two people with the gun and not actually fired it. So by that time, you must have considered the possibility of him doing so as unlikely."

"Yes, I suppose so."

"Good!" exclaimed the solicitor, "I have heard enough, if you agree I should be happy to take your case."

He stood up and held out his podgy hand.

"Well, OK!" agreed Ella hesitantly and took the proffered hand. There didn't seem many alternatives.

"I have a lot of reading to do," he said, beaming, "But I hope to see you again tomorrow, but let me know if they intend to interview you again before then."

He passed her his business card and with that he marched to the door and shouted that he was finished. The policeman standing outside opened the door and let him out.

Ella sat alone again in her cell. She had to admit she did not feel particularly reassured. She just hoped that she had not made a big mistake.

Two floors above, Gareth Anderson was staring at the bulky, surly figure of Bill Murphy. Murphy had been Bill Morrison's main enforcer. He had the battered face of the ex-boxer that he was and he was well hardened to police questioning. Gareth was therefore not getting very far, except that Murphy had supplied alibis for both the attack on Rachel Silverman and the break-in at Kevin's. Paradoxically, it was this that convinced Gareth of Murphy's guilt. An innocent man would have been hard put to remember where he was on one day over a week ago, but remembering, off pat, where he was on both days, one three weeks ago suggested something prepared in advance.

Over all Gareth felt satisfied. With luck they could probably break the alibis - the same woman in each case. There were also forensics. Hairs had been found in Silverman's that did not match the occupant's. Even better at Silverman's, there were traces of blood that were not hers. It appeared that the assailant had cut himself, during the frenzied attack. Forensics should be able to help.

Thinking of forensics, they were taking their time over DNA samples for the Draper case. Samples had been found, several different hairs, which may or may not be significant, as they could have been picked up anywhere and, much more significantly traces of saliva, mixed with lipstick from his face. He had chased the laboratory manager earlier, but they had said that there was a procedural delay, but that there should be a result tomorrow afternoon. They were so much more pernickety over their quality systems these days - not really surprising after the embarrassments of the last few years.

Gareth decided to call it a day. He was feeling tired but also a lot happier than he had felt for a while.

He terminated the interview and left for his office. He never got there. A desk sergeant stopped him in the hall.

"I've been told to pass this on to you sir. There is a fire at the house belonging to the Drapers' – the prof who was murdered. The fire brigade is there now."

CHAPTER 25

It was with considerable trepidation that Kevin entered the Mathematics building. It was half past eleven on the Tuesday morning. He had just come, by bus, from the Bridewell police station in the centre of town, where he had visited Ella. Her spirits had been much higher than when he had seen her yesterday. Then she had been brooding on the years that lay ahead in prison. She had been feeling particularly depressed about it, as she had grave doubts about the lawyer that she had just taken on. Today, though, she said that she realised how lucky she was to be alive and to have Kevin.

Kevin was now, focussed on his own problems. He had not gone in on Monday, feeling that no one would object to him having one day off, but he felt that he had to show his face today. The first thing he must do was to thank Murdoch for pointing out to him where his real interests and duty lay. What was worrying him, though, was meeting Dr Grant. After what had happened on Friday and how could he face the man?

He went up the stairs and through the fire door and then turned left into the outer office. Sadie was sitting at her desk in front of her computer. Her face looked drawn and haggard. She looked up at him.

"Hello, Dr Hansen," she said and then she flushed as she remembered Kevin's role in the affair. She fell silent, clearly struggling and failing to find anything suitable to say.

This was the sort of situation that Kevin himself was not particularly good at and they both looked at each other unable to think of how to continue.

The tableau was disrupted by the door of the inner office opening and Richard coming out.

"Good morning, Kevin," he greeted, cheerfully, "Just the man, I want to see. Come in! Come in!"

"Take a seat," he said, indicating a seat at the table next to his desk, as he shut the door.

"First things first. How's Ella or should we call her Emma now?"

"She's bearing up well and she wants to remain Ella. And thanks for rubbing my nose in what..."

"Don't mention it," interrupted Richard, "I like your Ella, there is something about her. She's well worth standing by."

"Anyway, I am not so sure that the police are finding the case against her as open and shut as they thought."

"She does deny it, but she was caught with the murder weapon in her hand. What more could they need?"

"Motive! The classic three criteria required in the successful prosecution of someone for a crime are means, opportunity and motive. They have the first two, but what could have been her motive?"

"I have no idea. Does that mean that they won't be able to prosecute her?"

"Oh no! All they need is to have a reasonable motive that they can put to the court. It does not necessarily have to be true. And they have such a motive."

There was a short dramatic pause. Kevin looked expectantly at Richard and realised how drawn and haggard Richard appeared, compared to how he had looked on Sunday. He was speaking loudly and cheerfully, as usual, but there was definitely something forced about it.

"Basically, they are suggesting that she was a hit woman. That someone else put her up to it. That would make her motive money. The type of motive that any court would consider reasonable."

"But who on earth would hire Ella – or anyone – to kill the professor?"

"The police have one prime suspect to fit that bill." Richard paused dramatically, "Me! I gain a promotion, more money, more authority and Draper is not there to sack me as, is well-known, he intended to do."

Kevin blinked looking stunned.

"What! They have accused you of this?"

"Yes! Near enough. To be honest it has me a bit spooked."

"I'm not surprised," said Kevin, struggling to absorb this new information.

"I suppose you are the big winner from Draper's death," added Kevin, spontaneously, "Though, I must admit, I feel a lot more comfortable without him around."

Richard smiled. "No need to backtrack, when it comes to motives, I'm suspect number one by a long way."

For the second time, since arriving in the department, Kevin found himself reduced to silence, as his thoughts raced.

The situation was again saved by the arrival of a third party. This time it was Sadie, unusually she opened the door without knocking.

Tears were streaming down her face and she was clearly having trouble speaking.

"Oh God!" she finally exclaimed, with a laboured gasp, "There's been another tragedy, the Draper's house has burnt down and a body has been recovered. They think that it is poor Mrs Draper. One of my friends has just phoned me. She heard it on Radio Bristol."

"The poor woman." said Richard, "Just after getting rid of that swine. Sorry I shouldn't have said that."

"No," responded Sadie, "Don't worry. I had no illusions about the Prof."

All three fell silent, apart from some sniffles from Sadie. This time it was the entry of Jack Sullivan that broke the silence.

"Good morning, everyone. I hope that I am not interrupting. I have been ringing around those industrial contacts of Bill's for you, Richard, and I have had some funny responses. I think that we had better have a chat about it when you have a mo."

"Sorry Jack, but we have all just had a bit of a shock. I am afraid that I have to tell you that Draper's house burnt down last night and the police have found a body. The suspicion is that it is Mrs Draper."

Jack Sullivan whistled softly.

"Do they know how it happened?" he asked, and as everyone, silently shook their heads, he continued, "Well, it could have been an accident. She would have been upset and may have left the chip pan on the stove or something - or it could have been suicide."

Jack Sullivan pondered his own last remark for a moment. "Unlikely, by all accounts, Bill was not an ideal husband."

His hand scratched gently the bald dome of his head, finally saying almost to himself "Or it could be another murder."

Back in his office, Kevin sat back in his chair. He felt glad to be alone. It was now just twelve o'clock and he had only been in the department for half an hour, but already his mind was spinning from all the shocks that he had had. He was glad that he had brought some sandwiches, since it meant that he would not need to face the rest of the department in the tea-room.

There was a knock at the partially open door and in walked the very last person he wanted to see; Dr Douglas Grant.

Kevin felt himself sinking deeper into his chair, wishing that he could vanish into it. Grant looked pale and still had a plaster on his face, but he did look a lot better than he had on Friday night.

"Frankly!" began Douglas, "I have no idea whether to be angry with you or apologise for what I said on Friday night. You weren't to know what she was. Though you do know now and are still visiting her. At best, Kevin, you are being conned."

Kevin stared. He wanted to say something, anything. But no words would come into his mind.

"You haven't a chance have you," continued Douglas.

He suddenly stopped and sat down in the visitor's chair.

"Damn it! I'm sorry. You have to do what you think is right. I think maybe we should do some maths."

At the last remark, Kevin felt acute surprise and then, still wordlessly, he nodded.

Surprisingly, the afternoon went relatively well. It was like it had been before. Douglas' initiative would kick things off with Kevin at first feeling blank. Then he would start getting engrossed and joining in, making suggestions and proposals.

They played with the practical implications of their ideas. It was Kevin, who noticed that when applied to evolving systems natural coding and decoding behaviour arose, there could be implications for the abiotic origin of life. They went silent for a moment briefly after that. As they both thought of their late boss. Draper would have loved it.

CHAPTER 26

DI Gareth Anderson was feeling angry, very angry. He was struggling to control himself. It was not the first time that he had crossed swords with Ian McDonald, solicitor and self-publicist and on each occasion the puffed up little Scotsman had wiped the floor with him. It was happening again.

"You see Mr Anderson," the solicitor continued, in his soft Scottish accent, "There is a very real problem with the consistency of your case with the forensic evidence. But on the other hand that forensic evidence is entirely consistent with my client's statement."

"If, as you contend, she had fired the gun and then stood there until the others found her with the weapon in her bare hand, then her hand should have been covered with traces of powder burns, especially as the handle is quite badly damaged. But not a trace was found. Indeed, there were fresh traces of talcum powder on the gun consistent with someone wearing latex gloves."

"Your case would now have to be that my client shot the professor with gloves on, disposed of them so effectively that you could not find them and then, inexplicably returned to pick up the gun and wait for the witnesses to turn up. Not a scenario that I would feel comfortable putting to a jury."

Gareth had just had an extremely uncomfortable session with the assistant chief constable and he did not need this. However, it was hard to find an effective answer.

"There is always the possibility," intoned Gareth, authoritatively, but with a lack of inner conviction, "That even though she fired the gun, no trace would be left on her hand."

"And the jury would believe that," snorted McDonald, "If you persist in this charge, then I will insist on a test firing of that gun being carried out just to see how many powder burns would be found."

He then turned to DI Wilkins, not bothering to wait for any further

response from Gareth. Wilkins faced him his face blank and unreadable.
"Intent," intoned McDonald, "Is a very slippery customer, as I believe you have experience of detective inspector."
George Wilkins said nothing, only a tiny twitch in his cheek indicated that the barb had got home.
"You do your homework, Mr McDonald," he finally said with a slight bow to the small lawyer. "Archie McMillan incited some half-wit to kill a security guard at a warehouse they were burgling. He claimed that the perpetrator had done it without any warning to him. The jury didn't believe him and found him guilty of aiding and abetting, but on appeal the judges released him claiming that there was no evidence of intent. McMillan went on to rape and kill two young girls. I don't think that they will want to make the same mistake again."
Wilkins gave the Scotsman a hard challenging look.
Even McDonald seemed taken aback by the steely determination of the man.
"I would like to point out that there is no evidence that my client played any role in the murder, being present does not constitute an offence."
"But conspiracy to cause grievous bodily harm is." responded Wilkins, "And is normally considered a sufficient justification for a successful prosecution for aiding and abetting murder."
Wilkins paused, as if letting the apparent finality of his words sink in.

"If you don't mind Mr McDonald, I would like to have a short discussion with my colleague in private." Wilkins finally, rather unexpectedly added.
The lawyer nodded and withdrew.
As the door clicked shut behind the lawyer, Gareth turned quizzically to George Wilkins.
"He's thrown a fairly big spanner into your case," Wilkins began, abruptly and somewhat brutally.
Gareth felt taken aback, but he couldn't deny the truth of the statement.
"And a little bit of grit into mine." he continued.
"Yes," said Gareth, "But Douglas Grant reported one of the accomplices as saying that Barnes carried the gun that should make it cast iron. You must surely have statements from the pair of them confirming that. They'll want to pin as much as they can on to the others."
"They would," responded Wilkins, "If they were alive. Bill Baxter died of a drug overdose, the same day that Barnes and Masters disappeared. Ed White was knifed a few days later, probably as a revenge killing for the death of Ashton by one of his 'disciples' on the estate."
"We still have a case of course. But..." at this point Wilkins hesitated, "I want to let her go."
"What!" exclaimed Gareth.

Wilkins made a smoothing motion with his hands.

"Before you rip my throat out, let me explain. The big fish is Charlie Lomax. Now the best witness against him is Douglas Grant, but he doesn't know that. The only witness that he will know about is Emma Barnes. In fact, in court, she would probably be entirely useless, as she was doped up to the eyeballs at the time."

"You think that he will try a hit?"

"Oh yes, and then we will have him. At present, we only have one witness."

"Surely, he would not do it himself."

"No, but we will get the hit men. We think we know whom Charlie will use and we can follow them from our end to Bristol. We have an inside source on Charlie's organisation. We will be able to track them all the way back to him. He will be sown up tight."

"And if they get through to Barnes?"

"One less piece of trash to worry about."

Gareth lifted his eyebrows at that.

"And the Avon and Somerset force carry the can. I don't think so."

"You have no choice. Let's be blunt, your case has collapsed. McDonald should be able to get her out in a few days through the courts anyway. I could hold her on the Ashton killing, but I am choosing not to."

"The bastard!" thought Gareth.

"All right, I am a shit," said Wilkins, as if he had read his mind, "But you know what drugs can do. We want this man stopped and this is our best chance to do it. And take out a nasty couple of killers at the same time."

Ella stared at the little Scotsman.

"Surely, you're joking."

"No, I am very pleased to say that I am not. They are releasing you. Though they did warn that further serious charges may still be made against you and you will have to surrender your passport and remain in Bristol."

"No problem! I have no passport. But how on earth did you do it?" Ella felt light-headed, almost as if she was floating above the room.

"The Draper case was relatively straightforward. I simply pointed out to them that if you had shot Draper without any gloves on, your hand should have been covered in powder burns, but forensics found not a trace. This is consistent with your story, but totally contradicts any likely prosecution scenario."

Ian McDonald beamed with pride.

"I knew that I had them cold on that one and, unless they could come up with a different and reasonably plausible story, the charge against you would have to be dropped."

The little lawyer then slumped a little.

"I must confess though, I am surprised that the charge over the Ashton murder was dropped. I did point out that 'intent' was a very tricky point in law, but, to be honest, I was not too hopeful. I was also expecting them to cast up statements from your former associates against you. But nothing came. Instead, I was asked to withdraw and after a few minutes they came out and said that they were releasing you."

"As your representative, I must point out that I am a little suspicious and just feel that you are being set up for something, but I do not know what. I would, though, recommend caution in your actions when you are out."

Ella stared.

"I'm sorry, but I'm still having trouble taking this in. I was expecting to be inside prison cells for a long time."

"There is a further issue," the lawyer continued, "The press have worked themselves up into a frenzy. Your arrest was big news, your release will also be big news and I am afraid that they have got hold of some of the details of how you survived in that shaft. "

"As your legal representative, and as we have been warned that other charges may yet be brought, I strongly recommend that you make no comment at this stage. Since anything you do say could prejudice any future defence."

"Agreed." said Ella, "I shall just refer them to you."

The thought of her name splashed all over the papers had Ella concerned. They would be calling her 'The Cannibal'. She took a deep breath. She was far from out of trouble yet.

There was a knock at the door and the young female detective came in, with a WPC in her wake.

"Are you finished?" she asked, "Because you are now free to go. WPC Woods has your belongings here and we must ask you to check them and if you accept that nothing is missing, then to sign for them."

Ella opened the proffered plastic bag. It contained her maroon dress and the small, black eveningwear handbag that she had been carrying. She opened it and the ten pound note, powder pack and tiny hair brush that she had put into it, as she rushed around that night, looked back at her.

Suddenly, she was crying. It was uncontrollable. The others stood patiently waiting for it to pass.

"I'm sorry." said Ella finally, "It has all just been too much."

"That's OK," responded the young detective, surprisingly gently, "Perhaps, you would like to sit for a bit and have a cup of tea before you go outside. I am afraid that there is a bit of a media scrum."

"No, thank you." replied Ella, "I'm alright now, but first I must phone home and tell Kevin."

In fact, she felt much better. The tears had seemed to clear her head. She was able to think again.

On leaving the police station, Ella became aware of the intense media interest. They paused for a minute on the steps and Ian McDonald read out a very short statement, basically saying that it would be inappropriate to say anything at this time. Ella stood there, trying to maintain a neutral expression, as the cameras clicked and whirred. Then ignoring the shouted aggressive questions of the mobbing journalists and reporters, they made it to the solicitor's car.

McDonald edged the car slowly out of its parking place trying not to run down any overeager reporters.

"It's very tricky with the press," he said, "They don't like not getting a statement, but speaking to them can backfire. If it offends their perverted sense of right and wrong, then they can come out with the most vicious self-righteous attacks on you. Also nothing would please them better than to get you to admit to things that would totally sink you in court."

"Do you think that they'll try and follow us?" asked Ella.

"Probably some will, but they'll have a good idea where you are going anyway."

As they headed up Gloucester road, Ella looked at the now familiar shops and streets. It was so good to be back, but for how long. Surely, they would throw the book at her over the Ashton murder. She was stunned that they hadn't done so already. She didn't feel worried about the Draper murder, after all she knew herself that she was innocent. It was strange though, her gun had been used. It suggested a link to her, but she could not imagine what it was.

She thought then of what she would do. Presumably, the old job at the supermarket had gone. She had lied about her references and even her name. No one would want to take her on. The only option seemed to be to sit and wait until the police had decided what charges to bring. Maybe that was their idea to unnerve her. Now that she was out the thought of going back to jail seemed unbearable.

CHAPTER 27

The gloom of the Indian restaurant acted as a cloak to hide in. Ella had found a seat in the darkest corner. It was Wednesday night. She had returned the previous evening to a somewhat subdued Kevin. They had spent that evening alone together. They had not really been apart that long, but so much had happened that it seemed an age. As usual Kevin had been the one feeling guilty, as he felt that he had not supported her properly. Ella had to point out that she had made a tiny contribution to her current predicament and that the crisis was far from over.

The surprise invitation to come out for a meal had come from Richard Murdoch. He had said that there was someone that he had wanted them both to meet. Getting there without being followed had been a bit difficult. There had been still a small number of journalists outside Kevin's house. They had taken a taxi to a pub further down Gloucester Road, with a back entrance and gone straight through it. They had then changed their jackets for spares that they had carried in a plastic bag. They had then walked the back streets to get to the restaurant.

She and Kevin had arrived and were now sitting alone waiting for Richard Murdoch and his mystery companion. She sipped her lager, wishing the restaurant were even darker. So far, no one seemed to have recognised her. It was not for lack of publicity. The day's Western Daily Press had carried a massive picture of her and her lawyer on the front page. She felt very conscious of her broad distinctive face and splayed out hair. The sort of unusual face that people would focus on as they idly looked around a room. They had almost finished their first drinks, when Richard Murdoch arrived. Behind him came a woman hobbling on a stick.

Ella looked at her curiously. She was in her mid-thirties, with large dark eyes, a prominent nose and a slightly plump body with small breasts. Richard pulled out the chair for her and attentively helped her to sit down.

He then sat down besides Ella, his face alight with mischief. The mystery woman looked at them, apprehensively.

"You!" he said quietly, looking at Ella, "Are not the only one with secrets. I would like to introduce you to Rachael Silverman, the love of my life."

"Pleased to meet, you." responded Ella, holding out her hand, "I suspect you know who I am. Just call me Ella."

"And I'm Kevin... Kevin Hansen." stuttered Kevin, his face reflecting profound surprise.

Poor Kevin, thought Ella, he would have had no inkling that all was not sunshine and light between Richard and his goddess wife.

"I hope that I haven't shocked you." said Richard, with a concerned look at Kevin, "But I'm afraid that marital relations between Margaret and me had broken down long before I met Rachel. If it were not for the girls, we would make our separation official."

"Of course!" exclaimed Ella, rather more loudly than she intended. "You were the woman who was attacked - Rosemary's friend. But how are you?"

"Much better, but I was in hospital for three weeks. I had some internal injuries and a broken pelvis. I have just heard some good news from the police. They phoned earlier today to say that they have now charged someone with the attack. It does make me feel much safer."

"Richard has probably told you that a similar attack was attempted against me. Fortunately, Rosemary had become suspicious and phoned the police. A young constable arrived just in time."

"I never understood it," said Rachael, "I suppose I do have a Jewish name, but why pick on me. It's years since I have even attended synagogue."

"These people are evil cowards," Richard ground out angrily, "It was probably because you were a soft target; a woman living alone."

"Do you know that the police had even suggested that I was responsible, because I was a common link between both of you. They even hinted that I had paid Ella to shoot Draper or had even done it myself. Incidentally, why did the police decide that you hadn't done for the good professor?"

"I probably need to be a bit cautious, but let's just say that the forensic evidence was entirely consistent with my version of events, but not with theirs."

"Well, I expect to see more of the police over this. They have discovered the obvious glaring fact that I had the strongest motive by a long way."

"Please don't worry," said Rachael, in her warm affectionate voice, "I'm sure that they will have other suspects, as well."

"Well, I can't think whom, except..." Richard hesitated, "You know there was one strange thing. That morning after the killing, I went into the University. I suppose mainly to see Draper's now my office. I found Karen Reading going through his desk and I think that she had also gone through his filing cabinets as well. She was really embarrassed when I found her. She came out with some nonsense that she was trying to find something for Grant."

"Karen Reading, isn't she the daughter of the late Sir George Reading? I used to work for him. He was a shit of the first order. He fired me in the end, but said that I could keep my job, if I could 'entertain' him. I told him to stuff it and walked straight out."

As Rachael finished this revelation a silence fell on the little group.

"I suppose that is a sort of connection with me." said Ella, finally, "But I have only seen Karen Reading once."

"Hmm…. it was a few years ago. I don't see why it should cause an attack now."

"Unless, she is trying to keep Sir George's name clean," muttered Kevin, almost to himself.

At that point, the waiter intervened to take their orders and they had to turn their attention to the menu.

As they waited for their meal, Rachel told them about herself.

She had been married many years previously, but it hadn't worked out and they had divorced. Since then she had lived alone working as a secretary. She and Richard had met in the street, just after Richard had visited Kevin. The visit had been to return a thesis from one of Kevin's post-graduate students and had been the one and only time up to that date that he had been to Kevin's home. They began talking and Richard had suggested that they go for a cup of coffee.

Watching her talk, Ella could understand what Richard could see in her. Her face exuded vitality, with her big eyes rolling around the room. Her speech was animated and spirited. She couldn't help contrasting her with Margaret, who had come across as cold and obsessed.

As they munched into their poppadoms flavoured with a variety of spicy dips. Ella told them about her own history. She enjoyed the telling, but even among these people she found herself editing and adapting it. Some of it she found too painful and some revealed a side to her that she wanted to keep hidden even from herself.

Afterwards they all went back to Rachel's house. Just after arriving, Richard took a walk around the block on a reconnaissance mission and reported that there were still a couple of reporters outside Kevin's house.

"Oh dear," laughed Ella capriciously as she sipped at the coffee that Rachel had made, "It's such a cold night and it looks like they will have to wait a bit longer."

Rachel's house had generally the same layout as Kevin's, but was furnished more tastefully, with no clashing colours. However, she did have full bookshelves, in the recesses next to the chimneybreast of the sitting room. Ella glanced briefly at the titles. There were a lot of novels, some classic and some modern. There was also a rack of music CD's, mainly classical.

The overall impression was of a cultured woman. She was also proving tonight that she could be lively and good fun in company.

It was midnight by the time that Kevin and Ella got home. There were still two reporters there, but Ella remained stiff-lipped, as the tired newspapermen accosted them and tried to question them.

Inside, it did not take long for them to fall into each other's arms.

Afterwards, lying in bed, Ella thought again of Karen Reading. She had only seen her once briefly in the men's changing room after Draper's murder. But she would not forget that thin anguished face. She fell asleep with that face still hovering before her inner eye.

CHAPTER 28

Douglas Grant sat on the leather couch. The beautiful, big house was feeling more and more like a prison to him. It was Thursday night and he had managed to go into the University today. Kevin had arrived late, looking tired, but happy. At first Kevin was even slower than usual, but Douglas persevered. He just had to do the mathematics, anything else was too painful. They did not discuss Ella's release. Douglas did not know what to think of it. His desire for revenge had been sated that evening, as he had watched his enemies die. He had overeaten on revenge and the spiritual indigestion was a great dark knot on his soul.

Now in the evening, there was no escape. Karen sat on the other couch, silent, distant and remote, like a faraway star on a clear, frosty night. She seemed to have withdrawn completely into herself. All attempts to draw her out coming to nothing. She looked ahead staring in the direction of the great dark expanse of the empty TV screen. He knew, though, that she was looking at images and thoughts inside her head. They so dominated her, she could barely acknowledge the outside world.

For Douglas, there was a strong desire just to walk out, to leave this madness behind. To meet a woman, who would speak, act and laugh, as most people do. He did not, because he remembered the woman he had loved. It was an image he kept in the front of his mind. He had to believe that one day she would come back to him. In the meantime, he must patiently wait with only his faith and memories to sustain him.

She became conscious of his eyes upon her and threw him a wan smile, devoid of any meaning.

"Look Karen!" exclaimed Douglas, angrily, "Whatever is eating you up, you need to address it. It's destroying you and it is going to destroy us."

"You have no idea," she responded, reflecting his anger, "What can you know? For God's sake just leave me alone!"

At this she stormed out of the room, slamming the door behind her. Douglas winced. Why had he lost his temper, when she needed gentle handling? He was an idiot.

He sat for another five minutes, staring into space, at a total loss. Then he heard a distant voice.

Were Karen and Mrs Turner, the housekeeper, talking? He felt curious and got up and quietly opening the door walked into the hall. Karen was in the drawing room at the front of the house. The door was partly open. He could hear her voice, but no answer. She was speaking on the phone.

He stood in the hall, uncertainly. He could make out clearly what she was saying.

"Tomorrow," she said, "I must see you, as soon as possible. Yes, that should be OK. What was the address again – 36 Casey Avenue. Yes, I know the road, just up behind the Elxo garage near the bottom of Pig Sty hill. I will see you there at 10 o'clock."

There was a click as the phone went down. Douglas retreated rapidly back into the sitting room and sat down.

Karen walked in shortly after. Her face looked brighter. He had the distinct feeling that she had come to a decision.

"I'm sorry I shouted at you," she said, apologetically, "You've been so patient and don't deserve this. I hope I can come to a resolution. I probably won't like it, but I must face the truth, whatever it is. And when I know, I will tell you."

She kissed him lightly on the cheek and said that she had to go to bed.

Douglas sat again staring at nothing in particular. What was going on? He decided then that he would also go to Casey Avenue, tomorrow. He would have to be careful. He did not want her to see him. Was it morning or evening? Well he would go in the morning and if she did not show he would go again in the evening. He felt that it would be the morning, going in the evening would mean having to give him some sort of explanation.

Why did he want to go? To see whom it was she met. And also something else, her emotions were so strong and taut, he felt that she could do anything. He was worried for her and others.

He'd better let Kevin know that he would probably not be in until the afternoon. They had arranged to start a bit earlier and that would have to be cancelled.

Thursday morning moaned Ella to herself. Last night had been a good night, but it had been a late night. She reached out her hand to Kevin's naked body that lay next to her. This elicited a groan and then a sudden yell.

"Oh no! I promised Doug that I would be in for eight this morning and

now look at the time. It's already after seven."
He fell out of bed and banged and clattered his way through the upstairs landing into the bathroom.
Ella moaned again. Could he not have done it quietly? She swung herself out of bed and sat upright on the edge slowly coming round. The morning chill got to her and she became aware of her nakedness. She stood up and crossed the room to get her dressing gown from where it hung on the door. It was still dark outside with just a hint of dawn coming through the curtains.
She could do with a pee, but Kevin was in full occupation of the bathroom. She decided that a cup of tea would be the best option. She went downstairs and into the small kitchen at the back. She did not normally have tea until breakfast was made, but she could really do with some.
She wandered through into the tiny dining room. A red flashing light caught her eye. There was a telephone message. She pressed the play button and sat down to drink her tea.
"Hello, Kevin, Doug here. I'm afraid that I will not be in tomorrow morning something has come up. Hope to see you in the afternoon. Bye for now."
"Bloody hell!" thought Ella, all Kevin's rushing around was to no purpose. They should have checked the phone last night.
A few moments later, Kevin appeared only half-dressed. Ella smiled at him.
"Why don't you take those clothes off again," she said, cheekily, undoing her dressing gown and letting it fall open.
"What! Really Ella! I must hurry."
"No you don't. There was a message from Douglas Grant on the phone saying that he won't be able to make it until this afternoon. So you have no excuse."

DI Gareth Anderson walked into his office. It was already quarter past nine. It had been a bad morning. He had slept in and woken up with a thick head - probably a cold coming on. He was disconcerted to find DC Jane Kent already in his office along with a man who looked vaguely familiar. The man was short of slight build, with the few remaining stragglers of ginger hair, closely cut on his nearly bald head. From his appearance, he was probably in his late thirties or early forties.
Gareth apologised for his lateness, his good manners getting the better of his irritation at this invasion of his office. Jane Kent introduced the newcomer as acting detective sergeant Mike Wilson, who offered his hand to Gareth without rising from his chair.
"Apologies for not getting up, but it takes a little time." Mike Wilson said,

patting his left leg, which made an unexpected dull hollow noise.

"Mike Wilson! Of course, Operation Cleansweep! What brings you here? I thought that you dealt with old unsolved cases. The Draper case may be unsolved, but it is not that old yet."

"To be honest, I don't know what has brought me here. I received a call from Geoff Miller of forensics, this morning and he said that he needed to see the pair of us urgently. He couldn't get you, so spoke to your DC Kent. He said that he would be here by nine thirty.

"Forensics! Leaving his ivory tower and coming here! It must be important." Gareth exclaimed. Various reorganisations had, in his opinion, left forensics as a remote and difficult to access service. In his early days, it had been so easy to have informal chats with them and to have a casual bit of work done. Now though, it was all quality systems, any work had to be approved and planned in advance and no report was given until it had gone through the proper channels.

Their musings were cut short by a knock at the door. Geoff Miller was a short, stocky individual with close-cropped, dark hair, thin wire glasses and a distinct Birmingham accent. His clean-shaven, pale face wore a worried concerned look.

After Jane had organised coffee. They all sat down, Jane on a chair against the wall and the other two facing Gareth across his cluttered desk.

"Gentlemen – and lady – began," began Miller, his face looking serious, "As you know, it is of paramount importance in the forensic service that we follow our quality procedures to the letter. Any failure to do so could and probably would invalidate our evidence in court. This means that samples must be properly described and come from authorised sources. Now we have had some problems in the past due to certain investigating officers passing unauthorised – illegally obtained samples – to us under different descriptions, sometimes through a separate department."

He paused for dramatic effect, as if his words might mean something significant.

Gareth and Mike Wilson glanced at each other each reflecting back the others bemused and puzzled expression.

"I take it then, that no such thing has happened in this case." Miller finally said, as the silence stretched out.

"If you mean that Mike and I have colluded to feed your department misrepresented samples, then certainly not," said Gareth firmly, as Mike Wilson vigorously nodded agreement.

"Then how do you explain that a sample of DNA submitted by DS Mike Wilson referring to a case from 1992, is exactly the same as a sample that you submitted from the Draper case. It was pure luck that we noticed as we were running the samples on the same day. I had them rerun in case there had been a mix up."

"The sample that I'm waiting for was from a gob of saliva spat on to the body of a young man who had been shot dead in a wood, near Hartcliffe. The first shot had entered his abdomen and brought him down, two bullets had then been placed into his head, and the remaining contents of the magazine had been emptied into his chest and side. The attack showed a considerable level of hatred and emotion." Mike Wilson calmly stated, "I had been complaining to your people about how long it was taking."

Gareth didn't feel calm. Now that he had grasped what he and Wilson were being accused of he felt very angry.

"It sounds to me, Mr Miller, that your department has failed to handle important samples properly. Quite bluntly, I think that it is a damned impertinence to come in here and try to cover up your own incompetence by making wild accusations. Frankly, I am struggling to think of one good reason why I shouldn't just throw you out on your arse."

Miller's lower lip began to quiver.

"Rarely, have I been spoken to in such a manner. I have..."

"Wait!" Jane Kent's calm voice broke through the rising verbal storm, "I suggest that everyone calms down. There is another possibility that needs to be considered."

Three pairs of eyes turned towards her.

"Perhaps, the samples gave the same results, because the same person was involved in both murders."

Mike Wilson added to the defusing of the situation.

"It's certainly possible. The attack showed a high disregard for life. Whoever did it would be capable of killing again."

"I presume that the DNA profile that you got did not match any on the file." Gareth said, breathing deeply to control his temper.

"It did not match that of any criminal convicted in the last five years." Miller said.

"We obviously thought about the possibility that the same person had been involved in both cases, but I'm afraid that we have had so much trouble with falsely described samples that we considered that more likely. My apologies for jumping to conclusions, but you can appreciate that I had to be sure." Miller added apologetically.

"If it really is the same person, then they may never have been convicted of anything. Did it match any DNA profile left at any other killing?"

"We're checking that now." replied Miller, having the decency to blush, "I'll check to see how they are getting on. If you can excuse me."

Miller got up and left the room, pulling his mobile phone from his pocket as he left.

Gareth took another deep breath as the door closed behind Miller.

"Thanks, Jane," he said, "I'm afraid my temper got the better of me, but what cheek."

"It was certainly an odd conclusion to come to," Jane said, "They must be finding false descriptions a serious problem. It involves so much bureaucracy now. I suppose it must be a temptation for officers."

"Quite handy for finding out who your partner's lover is, as well," added Gareth, before he could stop himself and earned a reproving look from Jane.

"In my case," began Mike Wilson, thoughtfully, "They initially pulled in two other youths who had been having a feud with the victim. They were quite a brutal pair and had been involved with other violent incidents and carried knives, but had never been associated with firearms. One was subsequently sent to jail for GBH in a different case, but the other is still free and has had no criminal record, since the late nineties. He appears to be happily married and working as a delivery driver."

Geoff Miller re-entered the room, his face looking thoughtful.

"That DNA profile has turned up in other case even more recently. A sample was found on the body of that enquiry agent, Bill Harrison, but his death was classified as an accident. But the nature of the death required that some checks be carried out"

"Accident be blowed!" exclaimed Gareth, smacking the fist of his right hand into the palm of his left, "We have our link. That thug Bill Murphy, the one who worked over the Silverman woman, he was Anderson's employee."

Gareth felt elated. He felt that finally they were getting somewhere.

The telephone rang. It was from the surveillance team watching the hitmen from Manchester – they were on the move.

Douglas Grant could not believe it. The one day he was in a hurry and the car lets him down. He stared sadly at the little Peugeot. It had misfired badly, as he had started it. He knew the signs. Damned modern cars. There was something wrong with the engine management system. What a man with a modicum of knowledge and a screwdriver once could have sorted out now took high-tech equipment and a new multi-hundred pound black box. He would have to get a taxi. Karen had already left and he had been determined to get to her rendezvous before ten o'clock. However, he had just seemed unable to organise himself. It was twenty to ten and now the car had failed him.

The wait for the taxi seemed interminable. They had said that they could be there in five minutes, but it was a good ten minutes before it arrived. He sat down in the back with a sigh. He could have sat in the front and chatted with the driver, but he did not feel up to trivial conversation. He needed to be alone with his thoughts.

He stared out of the window looking at a bright autumn day. Little clouds scattered across the sky and crows wheeled overhead. He thought of the crows, living their own lives almost oblivious to the humans scurrying around on the ground underneath. They must have their own problems and crisis, but few crows or humans must have had to face anything like he had faced over the last few months - the murder of Mark, the dreadful revenge that he had taken and now Karen. She had been so distant and preoccupied over the last two weeks. Maybe at last he would find out why. The taxi drove only a few hundred yards, before coming to a halt in a traffic jam on the Downs. Inwardly, Doug groaned his own laxity and depression were coming between him and the decisive action that he should be taking. He stared forlornly at the cut grass, piles of leaves and half-naked trees of the Downs. He looked at his watch, it was five to ten.

"Five to ten," laughed Ella, looking up at the big clock on the wall of the café. She glanced round the table, Kevin looked a bit anxious, Richard Murdoch was looking distinctly happy and Rachael was wiping sleep from her eyes. They had phoned Rachael, after a very late breakfast and had found out that Richard was still there. So Ella had suggested that they play truant and go for a coffee at one of the many cafes on Gloucester Road.

"You are all very late for work, except me of course," she grinned, "I am afraid that I have been sacked."

"That's damned unfair!" protested Richard, "You have after all been released."

"Only on bail, but the main problem was the one or two porkies that I told during the initial job interview."

Ella was facing the window and she suddenly stopped and looked.

"Bloody hell! What is she doing here?" She exclaimed.

The others looked at her in surprise, but she was already rising from her seat.

"Excuse me," she said, "But there is someone I must catch." And with that she almost bounded to the door and out into the street.

Kevin blinked. What was she doing now?

"Come on!" exclaimed Richard tapping his shoulder.

"Rachel, could you please settle up. We should all be back in a minute." Richard added, already halfway to the door and almost dragging Kevin behind him.

Out in the street, Kevin could not see Ella, but Richard pointed to the opposite side of the road, where they could just see Ella turning left up a side street.

Richard leapt into the road almost getting run down, by a fortunately slow moving car and had to leap back again on to the pavement out of the way.

"Damn!" he swore, "We're going to lose her."

"Come on! Now!" And he dragged Kevin across the road as the traffic ground to a total halt due to some unseen jam, further down Gloucester Road.

They turned the corner, around which Ella had disappeared and looked up the steep hill of Casey Avenue. There was a man in a baseball cap speaking into a mobile phone about 30 yards ahead and much further ahead a woman pushing a pram laboriously up the hill, but apart from that no one. There were mature trees lined up between the edge of the pavement and the road, about 20 yards apart, which could just hide her and they waited for a moment to see if she would appear.

"Where did she go?"

CHAPTER 29

It was quiet in 36 Casey Avenue, after the noise outside that came up this bottom part of the street from Gloucester Road. The hall was heavily carpeted with a plain, rich maroon and a rather sumptuous red and gold wallpaper decorated the hall wall. Paintings in heavy ornate frames hung suspended from a dark varnished picture rail. They seemed to consist mainly of portly, naked, renaissance nymphs, bathing, talking, sitting, or coyly eyeing up satyrs playing pan pipes in a variety of classical settings.

Ella had seen her quarry vanish into here. The door had been closed, but not locked and Ella had stepped in after Karen Reading. The heavily piled maroon carpet ran up the stairs from which a sound of muffled voices seemed to come. For a moment, Ella hesitated, then she cautiously began to ascend the stairs. The eyes of the nymphs and satyrs seemed to follow her.

On the upstairs landing, there were three doors, one of which was slightly ajar and from where the voices seemed to be coming. She moved quietly towards it.

"I must know!" sounded an expensively trained woman's voice, "I must know about Daddy."

"You may not want to know." responded another woman, but speaking in a rich, husky tone, with only the hint of a Bristol burr.

"I saw two of the videos. You were in one of them. Daddy was in them both. But those poor girls, they were always so young. Did neither of you care?"

"To your father, nothing mattered except his own satisfaction. If it wasn't for fear of prosecution, I think that he would have gone for them even younger. For me, I was only doing a job. Your father was paying me well. I was the manager of Dream Properties – really his procurer. The company only had two properties – this one and the house next door. We would lure the girls next door through the running of a bogus model agency. The Job Centre never caught on to what we were doing. If it looked like we could get them to play, then we would bring them here. They were well paid and some came back. We had a couple of regulars. But of course, they would lose most of their attraction to your 'Daddy', once they lost that hurt innocence."

"It must have been a financial shock for you when Daddy died."

"Oh yes. It was his final inconsiderate act."

"So what did Draper pay you? Because that's where you went after Daddy died."

This final question was met by a prolonged silence.

"Oh come on Margaret, don't play coy with me. I spoke to his wife the night he was murdered. She told me that he was involved with you and you joined in some of the sexual humiliation he subjected her to. When Daddy died, you started with Draper. Was that just a job too? What was he paying you? It must have been a blow for you when that monster from Manchester shot him."

"It was to protect Richard's job," came a response finally. "Sometimes it was just him and I and sometimes Susan would join in. Not that she had any choice. But then your boyfriend started to make himself useful along with that half-wit Hansen. Poor Bill, he really didn't want to give me up, but for him his ambitions were everything. Richard had to go."

The last remarks were spoken in a voice that had gone cold and flat, as if all emotion and feeling had been drained from the speaker. Behind the door, Ella stiffened; she felt a crisis was about to break.

"What are you doing? For God's sake put that away."

"You really should keep up with the news, Karen. They've released Hansen's freak- they'll be looking for someone else now. You know - I really hate you, your money, your wealth, your Sunday school morality. You've never known what it was to be poor."

Ella crashed through the door and two surprised faces turned towards her. To her left was Karen Reading her face deadly white her eyes red-rimmed. To her right was Margaret Murdoch, holding a small handgun. Trying to weave, as she did so, Ella charged towards Margaret. The small gun swung in her direction and there was a loud bang. Something smashed violently into her left arm, but her momentum kept her going and she rammed into Margaret.

They both rolled in a heap on the floor. Margaret had lost the gun, but she used her hands like claws going for Ella's eyes. They slashed down Ella's forehead, just missing one of her eyes. Ella was having trouble with her left arm, which was not responding and despite her strength was struggling to protect herself from her frenzied, desperate assailant.

"Stop!" screamed a voice, piercing the cordite-laced air of the room. They both turned from each other and looked. Karen had picked up the fallen gun and was pointing it at them.

"I know how to use this," she said, "Now back off Margaret!"

"You wouldn't dare." snarled Margaret.

"Try me!" snapped back Karen.

Margaret glared. She seemed to be assessing how serious Karen was. She got up, edged round Karen, keeping her distance and making no sudden move, and went out the door.

"Good God," gasped Karen, "She would have killed me."

Ella pulled herself up into a hunched sitting position. The blood was streaming down from the gashes above her eyes and there was a red patch and on the upper left arm of her blouse.

"Watch out! She may have another gun stashed somewhere in here."

Karen bounded to the door and on to the landing.

"No, she has gone out the front." her voice sounded back into the room.

Ella inspected herself. Both eyes were still operating though one required a constant wiping away of blood that was pouring into it. The fingers of her left arm still worked and she could lift it, though the movement caused a raw stabbing pain. Maybe she had been lucky.

Karen came back in and helped her up, while profusely thanking her and expressing concern about her injuries. Ella took in the walls of the room. The nymphs and satyrs had given way to large Perspex covered Romanesque paintings, depicting various naked and nearly naked men, women and at least one obvious hermaphrodite in various sexual acts or displays of the genitals.

"Pompeii," she thought, irrelevantly. It was in a book on the lost city of Pompeii that she had seen similar pictures before.

"Let's get out of here," she said out loud, as she accepted a wad of tissues that had appeared from Karen's handbag.

After standing indecisively for a few minutes, Richard and Kevin began to move slowly up Casey Avenue. Richard kept swearing under his breath.

Suddenly, one of the doors, on the opposite side of the street and about thirty yards further up, opened and a woman rushed out.

"What the devil!" exclaimed Richard, "That's Margaret!"

They watched as she came down the street in their direction, before stopping at a parked car and starting to unlock it.

"That's her car!" said Richard, rushing across the road and shouting her name.

Kevin looked further up the street in the direction from where Margaret had come. Up beyond the house was parked a powerful looking motorbike with the driver still sitting on it. He could see that the engine was still running by the little puffs of dark smoke that occasionally appeared. Another motorcyclist in full kit, probably the pillion passenger, was walking down the road towards the house that Margaret had come from. One of his hands was in his pocket.

Douglas Grant thrust a tenner into the taxi driver's hand and told him to keep the change. After the disastrous jam on the Downs the taxi had made good time. He had asked to be dropped off further up Casey Avenue and was now rushing down watching the house numbers.

As he past number 46, he saw two figures coming out a house a little further down, one partially supporting the other. Karen he thought, the taller thinner one was Karen.

Walking ahead of him was a man in leathers and a motorcycle helmet. He stopped and reached into its pocket. Douglas gasped. The man was pulling out a gun. The motorcyclist was intent on the two women, who had just started to come down the steps, and was unaware of Douglas coming up behind him. The man raised the gun aiming at them. Douglas sprinted desperately and barged into the leather-clad figure. There was a loud bang as the gun went off and then the weapon flew from the man's hand as he hit the ground.

The first thing that Ella and Karen were aware of was the retort of the gun and a shower of pieces of masonry as the bullet sailed above their heads and shattered some of the stonework above the door. They turned to look to see the two men struggling on the ground.

"It's Douglas!" screamed Karen, "It's Douglas!"

She hurried down the steps to help, leaving Ella supporting herself on the balustrade.

Ella stared up and down the street. She was feeling dizzy. A man was running rapidly up the road towards her. It was getting more and more difficult to keep her balance.

She gradually sank into a sitting position and became aware of more people appearing – policemen, some armed.

Someone sat down beside her.

"Ella! Oh my God! Ella! What has happened are you hurt," sounded Kevin's desperate voice, his arms around her shoulders.

"Kevin, I am so glad it's you," she gasped, thankfully.

"Don't worry it's only a flesh wound," she added, incongruously. She felt herself trying to giggle at her own ridiculous cliché as she started to lose consciousness.

CHAPTER 30

They sat in the spacious comfort of Karen Reading's sitting room. The heavy, expensive carpet and the leather suite gave a warm hush to the room that was accented by the gentle chimes of an ornate, wooden clock that sat on the teak mantelpiece.

Ella adjusted the sling that held her left arm. The wound could have been much worse, but the bullet had chipped the bone, so it would take a little time to heal. Even now, two days after the event it felt very uncomfortable. She had spent the last two days in hospital, having the wound cleaned out, stitched up and checked for any complications and infection.

She looked around the room. With her on the smaller couch sat Kevin, his arm protectively around her. Rachel Silverman sat in one of the armchairs, her walking stick propped against one of the arms. Douglas Grant and Karen Reading sat together on the larger couch.

Karen's eyes were wet. She had been telling them about her father.

"I have to live with that," she concluded, "For me Daddy will always be a wonderful man who loved me, but I must also remember the terrible evil he did to others. Perhaps I just have to remember him as two separate people, the man I knew and the man so many others knew and suffered through."

She reached for Douglas' hand.

"Don't worry, I am at peace with him now."

Everyone sat in silence for a few minutes alone in their own thoughts. Ella thought of Mark Ashton. Was she two people, one who had helped kill a man of such virtue and one who could love and care like a normal human being? Perhaps the best way of thinking about it was that the second had grown out of the death of the first. No, death was too final a statement for that first person; she was still there, still part of what made her, but weakened by her new knowledge and self-awareness. She leaned against Kevin for comfort.

The long silence was broken by Richard Murdoch being ushered into the room by Mrs Turner. His face looked drawn and pale. Everyone looked at him expectantly. He had been visiting Margaret in jail. He briefly touched hands with Rachel and then sat down in one of the other vacant armchairs. Douglas asked him if he would like a drink and got him the whisky and water that he requested.

Richard took a couple of gulps and looked around at the circle of faces.

"She has told me a great deal. She may have told me everything," he hesitated for a moment, taking a further gulp of whisky.

"It started over fifteen years ago, when her father's business hit a bad time and she had to go to the local school. She didn't mix very well there. For a young maturing girl, it was a disorientating and lonely existence. There was a boy – one of the wild bunch. She let him into her heart and body. He treated it as a public joke. She said that she nearly committed suicide then. But then somebody else beat her to it. A fat abused girl hung herself and all her schoolmates found it immensely amusing. She vowed then that they wouldn't laugh at her like that. She would get even.

"She waited over a year – a year of jokes and humiliation. She avoided the boy concerned, made out that she had accepted the situation and moved on. It was easy to get a gun. It was a matter of contacting the right man, well away from her area. With her body, there was no difficulty in paying for it. A few private visits to him and the gun and ammunition were hers. Then she practiced shooting in a lonely wood."

"His name was Sean Murray. It was easy to get him alone. All she had to do was offer him more of what he had already had. They drove to woods near Hartcliffe together in his father's car. Instead of what he expected she pumped him full of bullets. She said that she hated him so much that she would have emptied another magazine into him if she had had a further one with her."

"The police never suspected her. Apparently, they detained two young men on suspicion, but they had to be released. Her father's business improved, she went back to private school and got a place at Durham University, where, of course, we met. They knew her as the ice-maiden, there. An ex-boyfriend of hers once had a private chat with me after I started going out with her saying that he thought that something was wrong with her. Of course, at the time, I put it down to sour grapes."

"Perhaps, I was not the success that she hoped that I would be. She wanted to live in a smart area away from the hoi polloi. Her expenditure plans constantly unnerved me and we had major rows about it. Then she got that job, 'manager of an estate agency' was the official title. It was at the time that our oldest girl started school and Margaret was determined that it would be a private school. Of course we all now know what her job for Reading involved, it was a mixture of high class whore and procurer."

Richard looked around the room.

"I never suspected. By this time we were not living as man and wife. It was the girls that held us together. I suspected lovers, I had no idea what was actually going on."

"Well, Sir George died suddenly, and his ever vigilant lawyer quickly terminated Margaret's employment. Then it became clear that my job was under threat. Draper never liked me. He saw me as a lightweight who was just wasting space in his department that he wanted for his own people. We all knew that Draper was treating his wife badly, but I don't think any of us realised how badly. The man was a cruel sadist, who sexually and physically humiliated her. He would bring in prostitutes to help him, until Margaret offered her services. Apparently, Sir George and Draper knew of each other's predilections, so Margaret had already been involved with some sessions with Draper and his poor wife."

"When Sir George died, then Margaret began doing more for Draper. Of course, he quickly realised her desperate position and began abusing her as well. I can't believe what she went through for my damned job and I was naïve enough to think that it was due to the union and recognition of my ability, especially when I was promoted to deputy head of the department."

"This cosy arrangement was broken, by the remarkably fruitful relationship that developed between Doug and Kevin. Draper had to decide between Margaret and his ambition. His ambition won and he told Margaret that he was getting rid of me. She tempted Draper down into the changing room by getting him to believe that she was prepared to go through further humiliation for him. Of course, he couldn't resist. Margaret had already set up Ella to carry the rap. Ella's appearance on the scene at the appropriate moment seemed a Godsend at the time."

Richard stopped for a minute and drained his whisky. Douglas quietly got up and moved to the drinks cabinet to prepare another one.

"When I heard the next part of the story, I found it hard not to hit her. As she spoke, I just had to keep telling myself that this was a very sick woman."

"When she had been working for Sir George she met Bill Anderson, a debt-collector and enforcer."

This brought a gasp from Rachel.

"I'm sorry Rachel, so sorry, but let me finish."

"Margaret became suspicious of me. She suspected that I had a lover. So she put Anderson on the job of tracking me and he confirmed her fears. Of course, she paid for Anderson in her usual way. His need was orgasms enhanced by partial strangulation; useful feature, when she felt she had to wipe her trail clean."

"Margaret claims that she asked Anderson to organise only a frightener for Rachel, but I'm afraid I don't believe her. I'm sure that Anderson's thug knew how to administer the severity of a beating to order and that what happened to you, Rachel, was what Margaret had requested. She says it was because she thought that I would abandon her, leaving the girls in the lurch, but I think that in her own warped way she was jealous of Rachel."

"I think that view was confirmed by the speed with which she transferred her hatred to Ella. Anderson's information suggested to her that I was now having an affair with Ella, while Rachel was in hospital. We weren't by the way."

"So the same fate was arranged for Ella. But this time, due to an alert neighbour, it went wrong and the thug was lucky to escape. However, he had been through the house and found the gun, which he passed on to Anderson, who in turn passed it on to Margaret."

"Using that gun for the shooting of Draper made it appear a cast iron certainty that Ella would be convicted for his murder. In passing the gun to Margaret, Anderson had signed his own death warrant. He was now the only one, who could connect her with the gun. At their next session together, Margaret just continued the strangulation until he was dead and then set it up to appear like an autoerotic accident."

"Finding the gun made Margaret extremely curious about whom Ella really was. I had already told her the story about how Kevin had met her and the location made the connection with the Mantree estate murder and the missing suspects. As an extra flourish she put the note with Ella's real name on it into Draper's pocket."

"There was one more person who could connect her to Draper and that was Susan Draper. That poor woman was now free of that monster, but she wasn't going to enjoy it long. Margaret paid her a visit and simply strangled her. She said that it was like putting a sick dog out of its misery, the woman put up hardly any resistance. She then set fire to the house to remove evidence of her crime and to destroy any incriminating videos that were lurking in Draper's collection."

"Margaret thought she was now in the clear. She was a bit unnerved to receive the phone call from Karen, but knew that there was a paper trail that could connect her to Reading and that the best thing to do would be to talk to Karen. After all, it would be in Karen's interest to keep quiet about it for the sake of the reputation of her dead father."

"However, when Karen revealed that she also knew of Margaret's connection to Draper, she decided there and then to shoot Karen and burn the house. Fortunately, that 'half-breed bitch' – Margaret's description – interfered and stopped her in her tracks."

"She had another gun in the car, which she was going to use on me when I shouted to her and then go back to shoot Ella and Karen, but then the police appeared and she surrendered like a lamb. I think she knew by then that the game was up."

"What can I say? My wife killed four people and had Rachel badly beaten up. She expresses no regret. She is frantic that I keep the girls at Blue Maids. It's so bizarre; she speaks to me as she always spoke to me, except that she is in a police cell."

Richard took a heavy gulp of the second whisky that Douglas had poured for him and leaned back in his chair. The colour had returned to his face and he looked a lot better than he had when he had just arrived. Now he just looked very tired.

Karen looked at Ella.

"You saved my life, but what brought you into that house?"

Ella felt her face getting a little hot.

"Well, Richard had told us about you going through Draper's desk and well – I'm afraid – that you were my prime suspect. When I saw you walking up Gloucester Road, I wanted to find out what you were up to. I'm sorry."

Karen laughed.

"A good job, you did suspect me or I would be dead. Oh! I was going through Draper's desk to find if there was anything linking him to Daddy. I already knew from what Susan Draper had said that they had been associated in the abuse that she had suffered. To be honest, at that stage I wanted to destroy any connection to protect Daddy's reputation."

"I would like to thank you, as well." said Douglas, "I'm not quite sure what to say about trying to kill you. Except that I'm sorry."

"I would probably have done the same in your position. I had taken part in an appalling crime." replied Ella, "If it's any consolation, I can't forgive myself for my part in it. But I believe that you also saved my life. The police would never have stopped Lomax's man in time, even though they were meant to be tracking him."

A silence fell over the small group.

Then into the silence came a sound as if someone in the distance were sawing wood. They all looked at Richard. The empty whisky glass lay on his lap and his eyes were closed, as he snored gently in the comfortable armchair.

The bright spring morning sun shone down from the white flecked sky. Ella was walking with her arm tucked into Kevin's through a sea of green and yellow. All around her spring was exploding into celandine and bursts of daffodils. Somewhere in the hawthorn hedge to her left a magpie screeched – raucous, but brief. The wood they were approaching was already decked in fresh spring green.

Far below, cars sped along the grey band of the M32 motorway, their roar quietly distant. Beyond through trees lay the houses and churches of Fishponds – a faint mist still clinging to them. Nearer glistened the flat, still waters of Duchess Pond. Scattered round its green perimeter were the huddled figures of fishermen.

Ella felt happy. Happier than she ever imagined she could be. Her body was rhythmically responding to the new melody within her, as an ancient, wondrous mystery began to unfold. She could feel the differences, the morning nausea had passed, but her nipples were prickling and her stomach was already starting to gently swell. The thought of that new life excited her in a way that she never dreamed possible. It was happening when and where she wanted. She felt both secure and in control.

For an instant, as they entered the wood, it seemed very dark and gloomy, before her eyes had responded to the lower level of light. There were certainly problems ahead. She would have to stand trial for possession of a firearm. Fortunately, the law had not yet changed to increase the severity of the possible sentence and the police had not added to the charge list. Ian McDonald believed that she should be able to avoid jail. Having Douglas Grant as a character witness would help considerably. There was also the trial of Lomax and his associates, in which she would have to appear as a witness. The tentacles of the past could still reach for her.

As her eyes grew accustomed to the lower light level, she became aware of snow flurries of white wood anemones, lying patterned over the ground between the trees. Shafts of light lanced through the trees catching flying insects as dancing specks. The whole wood seemed to glow with magic, as new life overpowered the winter's death.

She stopped and looked into Kevin's face, his eyes shone back. His shyness was still there, but the pain and uncertainty had gone.

They embraced and melted into a long kiss.

ABOUT THE AUTHOR

Owen Chambers has been an industrial chemist throughout his working life. He has worked particularly in the manufacture of inhalation anaesthetics. Until 2005, he worked in a factory environment and, since then until present, he has been working as an independent consultant.

He was born in Scotland in 1950 and currently lives near Bristol in the UK. He is married with three sons.

He enjoys reading and particularly enjoys mystery stories and science fiction. His favourite authors are Isaac Asimov, Agatha Christie and Iain Banks.

This is his first book, which he very much enjoyed writing.